Acclaim for Christa Faust's MONEY SHOT...

"*Money Shot* is a stunner, careening along with a wild, propulsive energy and a deliciously incendiary spirit. Laced with bravado and loaded up with knockabout charm, Christa Faust's Hard Case debut is the literary equivalent of a gasoline cocktail."

—*Megan Abbott*

"I was sucked into the tight, juicy *Money Shot*, from the ripping car trunk start to the hard-pumping climax. This novel is so convincing that you want to believe Faust has been an oversexed, naked killing machine, at least once."

—*Vicki Hendricks*

"*Money Shot* is smart, stylish, insightful, fast-paced pulp fiction with razor sharp humor and a kick-ass heroine. Christa Faust is a super crime writer."

—*Jason Starr*

"*Money Shot* makes most crime novels seem about as exciting as the missionary position on a Tuesday night. The results are stunning."

—*Duane Swierczynski*

"Wonderfully lurid, with attitude to spare and a genuine affection for the best of hardboiled traditions. Christa Faust is THE business."

—*Maxim Jakubowski*

"Christa Faust writes like she means it. *Money Shot* is dark, tough, stylish, full of invention and builds to one hell of a climax."

—*Allan Guthrie*

"Christa Faust proves she can run with the big boys with this gritty thriller set in the darkest places of the porn industry. I loved it!"

—*McKenna Jordan, Murder By the Book*

"Never has an avenging Angel been sexier. *Money Shot* leaves you spent and wanting more."

—*Louis Boxer, founder of NoirCon*

"Sam?" I called when I got to the top of the steps.

"Come on in." Sam's voice came from the far end of a long hallway.

There was a partially open door with a bright light inside and I walked toward it. There were no fat yellow cords duct-taped to the floor, no adjacent rooms full of giggling girls powdering their implant scars and gluing on false eyelashes. There was no one hanging around smoking or talking on a cell phone. Just that long empty hallway. I like to think I was starting to wonder a little at that point, but I didn't leave. I just pushed the door the rest of the way open and went right in.

The room at the end of the hall was mostly empty, except for a large wrought-iron bed with a bare mattress covered in plastic. Sam stood against the far wall, beside an empty fireplace. There were two other men I didn't recognize, but I didn't get much of a look at them because Jesse was right by the door looking delicious, dark hair tousled and blue eyes smoldering, ready to go. He wore leather pants that hung so low on his lean hips that you would have seen his pubic hair if he hadn't shaved it off. His sleek, lanky torso was bare and sheened with sweat that highlighted the symmetrical perfection of every muscle. He stepped up to me, gave me an appreciative once-over and smiled.

"Angel Dare," he said. "Wow. You look amazing. This is gonna be awesome."

Then he punched me in the face...

SOME OTHER HARD CASE CRIME BOOKS YOU WILL ENJOY:

MONEY SHOT

by **Christa Faust**

A HARD CASE  CRIME NOVEL

A HARD CASE CRIME BOOK
(HCC-040)
First Hard Case Crime edition: February 2008

Published by

Titan Books
A division of Titan Publishing Group Ltd
144 Southwark Street
London
SE1 0UP

in collaboration with Winterfall LLC

Author photo by Jim Ferreira

Print edition ISBN 978-0-85768-346-5
E-book ISBN 978-0-85768-392-2

Cover design by Cooley Design Lab
Design direction by Max Phillips
www.maxphillips.net

Typeset by Swordsmith Productions

Printed and bound by CPI Group (UK) Ltd, Croydon, CR0 4YY

For Richard S. Prather

Words don't die.

MONEY SHOT

1.

Coming back from the dead isn't as easy as they make it seem in the movies. In real life it takes forever to do little things like pry open your eyes. You spend excruciating ages trying to bend your left middle finger down far enough to feel the rope around your wrists. Even longer figuring out that the cold hard thing poking you in the cheek is one of the handles of a pair of jumper cables. This is not the kind of action that makes for gripping cinema. Plus there are these long dull stretches where people in the audience would probably go take a piss or get popcorn, since it looks as if nothing is happening and they figure maybe you really are dead after all. After a while, you start to wonder the same thing yourself. You also wonder what will happen if you throw up behind the oily rag duct-taped into your mouth or how long it will take for someone to notice you're missing. Otherwise you are mostly busy bleeding, trying not to pass back out, or laboriously adding up the cables, the stuffy cramped darkness, the scratchy carpet below and the raw hollow metal above to equal your current location, the trunk of an old and badly maintained car. That's what it was like for me, anyway.

I'm sure you're wondering what a nice girl like me was doing left for dead in the trunk of a piece of shit Honda

Civic out in the industrial wasteland east of downtown Los Angeles. Or maybe we've met before and you're wondering why it hadn't happened sooner.

My name's Gina Moretti, but you probably know me as Angel Dare. Don't worry, I won't tell your wife. I made my first adult video when I was twenty, though I lied on camera and said I was eighteen. It was volume one of Marco Pole's now-famous amateur line, *Brand Spankin' New*. My scene was just one of five but there's no question that I stole the show. What can I say? I know where my strengths lie. I had a contract with Vixen Video less than two weeks later and before I knew it I was on the Playboy Channel doing soft-focus video centerfold segments for more money than I earned in a year back home. A porno Cinderella story, but unlike so many of the girls I worked with, I was smart enough to stay off drugs, save every penny, and get out before my pussy turned back into a pumpkin.

Problem was, I just couldn't stay retired. Like a pro wrestler or a jewel thief, I was a sucker for an encore. I had no idea when I said yes to Sam Hammer that I'd end up stuffed in a trunk.

Sam's an old friend. One of the few genuine good guys left in the biz. Kind of a cross between Santa Claus and John Holmes. He must have been pushing sixty, burly and cheerful with a silver ponytail and neatly groomed beard. He was the kind of guy that always had a sofa to crash on or a shoulder to cry on, a loan till your next check or a guy he knew who would fix your toilet for cheap. I'd say he was like a father to me, but that would sound kind of weird since we did a few scenes together, back before he started working exclusively behind the camera. Never mind how long ago. He had been a perfect gentleman too, easygoing, respectful and reliable as clockwork. No easy feat before Viagra became the backbone of the industry, so to speak. Back when you actually had to count on feminine wiles to make the trains run on time, a man like Sam who could stand and deliver on cue was worth his weight in gold. Now you have guys popping Viagra and Cialis like tic tacs and shooting Caverject directly into the equipment to get things up and running. Better loving through chemistry.

Sam Hammer shoots were always a blast. No pressure. Sam was married to all-natural triple-D legend Busti Keaton, star of the *Topsy Turvy* series and *Battlestar Gazongas*. She would cook huge amounts of the best down-home comfort food and fuss around the set making sure nobody was too hot or too cold or uncomfortable in any way. I've been on plenty of jobs that were just jobs, or worse. Hammer shoots never felt like work. More like big happy Sunday barbeques where they just happened to be filming people having sex.

Sam could have easily made the jump to Hollywood. He had a great eye for composition and wrote witty, original scripts that actually kept your finger off the fast forward button. But we all knew that he would never leave the Valley. Sam was a lifer. He liked being around naked girls way too much to go legit. So many smut directors are nothing but jaded hacks who spend most of the shoot snorting lines or talking on their cell phones, but not Sam. His enthusiasm was infectious.

When he called, I was having one of those days. Those sneaking-up-on-forty days when I can't stop looking in the mirror. Comparing what I see now to the image of that perfect, flawless little twenty year old bouncing around on top of Marco Pole for digital eternity. I'm in better shape now than I ever was, working out six days a week and kickboxing to knock out stress, but all the crunches in the world can't reverse gravity, or crow's feet, or the fact that I have to use the hair dye that advertises "100% gray coverage!" Don't get me wrong, I've got a pretty iron-clad ego, but I run Daring Angels, a high-class adult modeling agency out in Van Nuys, and being around all those gorgeous nineteen-year-olds sometimes gets to me. Makes a girl feel like yesterday's news.

When Sam called, I was standing in the full-length mirror beside my desk, topless and sideways. I have always been proud of the fact that I never had my tits done. I've seen way too many beautiful women ruined by ghastly, wall-eyed Frankenstein implants. Yet, on that day, I was hefting my assets in the palms of my hands and wondering if maybe they could use a little surgical pick-me-up after all.

I called my receptionist, personal assistant and all-around Mom Friday into my office. Didi was big back in the *Deep Throat* days, though if you saw her now, you'd never know it. She was fifty-two, five feet even, with a plain, sweet face like your favorite teacher, but underneath that G-rated exterior was an old-school porn veteran who talked about sex like other people talk about the weather. She had a rich, phone-sex purr of a voice and she got asked out on dates nearly every day by the men who called to book girls. More than half of the time she said yes, and though they may have done a double take when she showed up, I doubt any of those guys were sorry by the end of the night. Didi was probably the best thing that ever happened to me. I don't even want to think about how I would have run Daring Angels without her.

She came in the door with her sparkly vinyl purse on one arm and the other arm sliding into the sleeve of her pink leather jacket.

"What's up, boss?" she said. "I'm just out the door. Got a hot one lined up tonight." She looked down at my exposed breasts and rolled her eyes. "Would you stop it already! You do *not* need a goddamn boob job."

I grinned. "Go on, Didi. I'll see you tomorrow."

She blew me a kiss and split. I turned back to the mirror. I knew she was right, but still…

When I heard my phone's electronic chirp, I jumped a little, feeling like I'd been busted somehow.

"Daring Angels," I said.

"Angel, baby." Just hearing Sam's familiar growl was enough to cheer me up. "How you doing, beautiful?"

"Never better," I replied, turning away from the mirror and grabbing my push-up bra off the back of my chair. "You?"

"The usual," he said. "You know. Making dirty movies."

"How's Georgie?" I asked, holding the phone between my cheek and shoulder and hooking the bra around my ribs.

Georgie was Busti Keaton's real name. I should have noticed the tight little pause and the pinched tension in his voice as he answered much too quickly.

"Fine, she's real good. Listen, Angel, I got a favor to ask."

"Anything, Sam," I said, turning the bra around and slipping my arms through the straps, settling everything into place. I eyed my reflection. Much better.

"I'm shooting with Jesse Black," Sam told me. "I had a new girl flake on me and we've only got the location for another two hours."

I nodded and leaned over my laptop, calling up my booking calendar.

"Okay," I said scanning the schedule. "Zandora Dior and Kyrie Li are both out of town featuring, but Sirena, Coco Latte and Roxette DuMonde are available, or I've got this new kid, Molly May. She's a knockout, a legit redhead—carpet matches the drapes. Fresh, petite girl-next-door type but she also glamours up real nice. She's only a B-cup, though. It's not a busty line, is it? Bethany Sweet is my only current double-D and she's booked today."

"Actually," Sam said. "Jesse asked for you."

"Come on," I said, laughing nervously and turning back toward the treacherous mirror. "Sam, you know I'm retired."

"Angel, please, I really need your help on this. Jesse is threatening to walk out on me and I promised him I'd get him any girl he wanted. He wants Angel Dare. He says he cut his teeth on your movies, that you were his favorite since he was fifteen."

Now you have to realize that Jesse Black was probably the hottest new male talent in the biz. He was twenty-one, Hollywood handsome and legendary below the belt. The bluest blue eyes. Bad boy smile. More than half the women who who'd come to me looking for work in the past six months said they got into porn specifically because they wanted to work with Jesse Black. Now Jesse Black wanted to work with me.

"It's pretty short notice, Sam," I said, already finding

my mind shamelessly wandering over the details of Jesse Black's famous anatomy.

"No anal," Sam replied. "Just a simple little boy/girl scene with a facial pop. I can give you fifteen and a cover. It'll be like old times."

I had to admit it was appealing. It'd be a phone-in, plus Jesse Black, plus helping Sam, plus an easy fifteen hundred bucks and a big fat box cover ego boost. Proof I've still got it. I could feel my resistance wearing down fast, but I had to keep trying.

"I don't have a current test," I said. "It's been almost seven months."

"You can just fax it in to me by Monday," Sam said. "Look, I'll make it two grand."

"Sam...I..."

"Okay, twenty five, what do you say? I'm in a jam here, Angel. My last three videos tanked and if I screw this one up too, I'll probably get shitcanned from Blue Moon. But with Angel Dare and Jesse Black on the box cover, I got a sure thing."

He was starting to sound desperate. If it had been anyone else, I probably would have held my ground, but Sam had always been there for me whenever I needed anything. No questions asked.

"Okay, Sam," I said. "Jesse knows I'm condom only?"

"Sure," Sam said. "It's no problem. Look, I'll put him on, okay?"

"Wait," I said but it was too late.

"Angel?" a new voice said. "Is this Angel Dare?"

"In the flesh," I said. "This Jesse?"

"Yeah," he replied. "Angel Dare, wow. I can't believe it's really you."

"It's me alright," I said, having no idea what else to say.

"God, you're so hot," he said. "I swear I must've worn out, like, three copies of *Double Dare*. That scene you did with Nina Lynn in the shower." He made a breathy little purring noise. "Damn."

"Thanks," I said, eyeing my reflection again. Back when I shot *Double Dare*, Jesse probably still thought girls were icky. It seemed so wild that a toddler like him would have the hots for me. "You're not so bad yourself, kid."

"Will you do it?" he asked. "Please say you'll do it. It'll be like my best fantasy come true. Me and Angel Dare."

"Well..." I said.

"I'll make it good for you, Angel," he said, voice raw and earnest, like my first boyfriend. "I promise."

"Put Sam back on, okay?" I said.

There was some quick shuffling and then Sam's voice came back on the line.

"Come on, Angel," Sam said. "Make the kid's day. He's gonna start humping me if you don't get here soon."

I sighed and grabbed a pen.

"What's the address?"

2.

The location was one of those sad old mansions in Bel Air. Ostentatious, but had seen better days. Money is so fickle here in L.A. and a big old house is like an aging mistress with a plastic surgery fetish. It's more economical to just buy a cheap, flashy new one than keep on renovating the old one. Otherwise, you wind up renting the place out for porn shoots just to break even on the roofing bills.

There was a pair of twisted pomegranate trees guarding the open gate and the ground beneath them was gory with broken crimson fruit that crunched and splattered under the wheels of my little black Mini. Pulling into the wide circular driveway, I kept expecting to spot Norma Desmond burying her pet chimpanzee in the overgrown rose garden. I felt better once I saw Sam's red '84 Corvette with its vanity plates that read HAMRXXX. It was parked near a massive wooden door that looked like it ought to open into a medieval Spanish dungeon. I parked behind Sam and got my old shoot bag off the passenger seat. There were a few other cars I didn't recognize in front of Sam's, a generic mid-sized rental and a tricked out, over-the-top black Ferrari that had to be Jesse's. Car like that just screamed dick-for-hire. Parked directly in front of the Ferrari was the battered blue Honda Civic with which I would soon become so intimately familiar.

I've spent a lot of time since then going over and over those short minutes in the driveway, wondering why I didn't sense something wrong, why I just waltzed right in like some barely legal bimbo from Indiana. I try to tell myself it was because I trusted Sam, because he was my friend for nearly twenty years, but if I'm honest I have to admit that was only part of it. The simple truth is, I had a girl boner. All the blood had run out of my brain and down between my legs. I'd had this semi-regular thing with a rockabilly bass player that had lasted nearly six months, but it had recently gotten stale and predictable and I'd decided it was time to move on. It had been three weeks since I'd gotten any new action. Now I found myself in a ditzy hormonal fog, gone blonde at the thought of putting Jesse Black's lean, hard, twenty-one-year-old body through its paces. So I walked, crotch-first, right into a trap.

The wheels of my little roller suitcase bumped along over the cracked pavement and the lonely echoing sound seemed way too loud in the deserted courtyard. The door wasn't locked. I thought they might be shooting some dialog or pick-up footage so I didn't knock. I just slipped quietly inside.

The first thing I noticed was that there was no furniture. It was a huge, hollow room with a cathedral ceiling, Spanish tile floors and a massive iron chandelier on a chain that looked like something Zorro would use to swing over the heads of the bad guys. There were several large windows, but they were covered with opaque plastic, letting in only a soft, muted fraction of the afternoon sun. It smelled like fresh paint.

"Angel?" Sam's voice called from the top of an elegant, curving staircase. "That you?"

"Yeah," I replied, squinting up the stairs.

"We're up here," Sam said.

I pushed down the telescoping handle on my case and hefted it to carry it up the stairs. Luckily, it was just the small shoot bag and nearly empty. Sam said I'd only need lingerie and heels so I had run by the house on my way over and thrown together a couple of sets and stockings to give him some options. It's been years since I had my shoot bags packed and ready all the time, everything organized into neatly labeled Ziploc bags and categorized with titles like *fetish*, *slut*, or *GND*, which stood for Girl Next Door.

"Sam?" I called when I got to the top of the steps.

"Come on in." Sam's voice came from the far end of a long hallway.

There was a partially open door with a bright light inside and I walked toward it. There were no fat yellow cords duct-taped to the floor, no adjacent rooms full of giggling girls powdering their implant scars and gluing on false eyelashes. There was no one hanging around smoking or talking on a cell phone. Just that long empty hallway. I like to think I was starting to wonder a little at that point, but I didn't leave. I just pushed the door the rest of the way open and went right in.

The room at the end of the hall was mostly empty, except for a large wrought-iron bed with a bare mattress covered in plastic. Sam stood against the far wall, beside an empty fireplace. There were two other men I didn't recognize, but I didn't get much of a look at them because Jesse was right by the door looking delicious, dark hair tousled and blue eyes smoldering, ready to go. He wore leather pants that hung so low on his lean hips that you would have seen his pubic hair if he hadn't shaved it off.

His sleek, lanky torso was bare and sheened with sweat that highlighted the symmetrical perfection of every muscle. He stepped up to me, gave me an appreciative once-over and smiled.

"Angel Dare," he said. "Wow. You look amazing. This is gonna be awesome."

He reached down and squeezed his most famous feature through his tight leather pants. Then he punched me in the face.

3.

I wasn't out cold, but it hurt like hell and everything went red and swimmy. I could feel rough hands on my body, wrenching my clothes and throwing me down on slick, crinkly plastic. Scratchy rope around my wrists and ankles and my first semi-delirious thought was, *Bondage, are they crazy? You can't shoot bondage and sex in the same scene!*

Then the pain kind of tightened and focused down to a nasty throb in my left cheekbone and temple and I was able to see again, to put my mind to the task of moving beyond the *holy shit* phase and into working out exactly what sort of trouble I had gotten myself into. I should have known something wasn't right about this set-up as soon as Sam gave me the Bel Air address. Nobody in porn ever goes over the hill for anything if they can help it.

Near as I could figure, I was tied in a sloppy and unimaginative spread eagle, face up. My shirt and bra were shoved up under my chin and my skirt was torn up to the waist. I had no idea what had happened to my panties. Jesse stood over me to my left with the kind of lobotomized expression men get when they have their hands in their pants. Behind him was one of the two strangers. Thick and dead-eyed with skin the color of boiled potatoes and a build like a rhino on steroids. He was wearing tight leather gloves and did not have his hand in his pants. He had Sam by the arm, holding him near the bed like a naughty kid about to be punished.

"They have Georgie," Sam said, his voice barely audible. "I'm sorry."

The rhino gave Sam a casual cuff to the side of the head that would have knocked him to the ground if the guy hadn't been holding him up.

"Jesus!" Sam said.

"Shut up," the rhino said, mildly, like he was ordering a beer.

Sam squeezed his eyes closed and hung his head.

I was about to say something really stupid that involved the rhino's mother when the other guy came forward, sliding slowly into view on my right. I knew then that the rhino was the least of my worries.

This guy was the type you don't even see. Invisible, just a guy like a hundred other guys. Medium build, brown hair, forgettable features above a forgettable shirt and a forgettable tie. But once you did notice him, once you saw past the bland, everyman veneer, once you looked in his eyes, you saw this was a very bad man. He gave off a powerful alpha vibe that all the other men in the room deferred to without hesitation. There was no question that he was the boss.

"Where is the money?" he asked.

I didn't even bother to say *what money* or anything at all. I just squinted at him, silent and furious and wondering what it was going to take to get out of this in one piece.

The boss tilted his chin toward me.

"Ask her," he said.

Jesse smiled and gave me a tight right to the belly.

I had a few panicked seconds where I was sure I was about to puke. My body fought to curl up around the pain, but my limbs were tied so I stayed splayed, drowning in nauseous agony.

"I don't know what you're talking about," I said, or tried to. What came out was more of a breathless wheeze with no consonants.

"A girl came into your office with something that didn't belong to her," the boss said. "A briefcase. She left without it. It isn't anywhere in your office or your house. Where is it?"

It all came back to me in a sickening rush. That girl. The anxious blonde with the Dracula accent who came to my office just before lunch, about six hours before Sam's call. The one who was looking for one of my models, Zandora Dior.

"Lia," she said her name was, sitting there on the other side of my desk and seeming lost inside an extra large Lakers t-shirt.

Her big green eyes were evasive, her body language tense and urgent. Her frosted blonde hair was obviously expensive, and her thick fake nails were fresh and glossy, but her body was undernourished, toneless and skinny-fat and her skin was bad, broken out around her tiny rose-bud mouth. She wore no make-up but I could tell that she would still doll up well enough to shoot for another six months or so. The t-shirt was as long as a dress, nearly covering the tight black skirt beneath and making her look like she had forgotten her pants. The briefcase sat between her big feet. I barely noticed it.

"Do you have ID?" I had asked her, sizing her up,

looking at her pale, childish legs and the expensive high heels that were way too dressy to go with the t-shirt. I saw nothing but trouble. "I can't even take test shots of you if you don't have an American driver's license."

"I am not wanting work," she said. "I am wanting Lenuta Vasilescu. In the movies, she is Zandora Dior."

I looked the girl over again, wondering what this was all about.

"Zandora's featuring," I said.

Lia frowned like she had no idea what I was talking about.

"She's out of town, featuring." I elaborated. "You know, dancing. On the road."

"When will she be back?" Lia asked.

"Monday," I replied.

"Oh," Lia said, looking down at the briefcase and twisting her skinny fingers in her lap like a child. "Can I please have her phone number? We are friends together as children in Brasov. It is very important. I need to speak to her right away."

Maybe because she knew Zandora's real name, or because she was obviously Romanian too, or maybe because she looked so small and desperate, like a bird with a broken wing, I impulsively felt like helping her out. There was no way in hell I was going to give her Zandora's private cell number, but I also wasn't going to just tell the kid to fuck off with her sitting there looking like she was trying really hard not to bust out in tears.

"Do you want me to give her a message?" I asked.

"It's..." The girl swallowed hard and looked away. "It's private."

"Tell you what," I replied. "Why don't you write her a

note with your phone number and whatever else. I can fax it to the club Zandora's booked at and then she can call you."

"Okay," Lia said. It was clear that she was not happy about it, but in too much of a hurry to argue. "Can I have paper?"

I gave her a blank sheet out of my printer and a sparkly purple Daring Angels pen. She leaned over my desk and wrote fast and hard, like she was trying to engrave the words into stone. She was clearly writing way more than a phone number. In fact, I didn't see anything that looked like a phone number at all. Just a crowded block of looping, girly script infested with strange hooks and squiggles. Even upside down, I could see she wasn't writing in English.

I felt a little weird sending Zandora a note I couldn't read, but after all, it was only a note. Even if it turned out to be some crazy stalker shit or who knew what else, Zandora didn't have to respond. It wasn't like I was giving the girl Zandora's number or even letting her know which club would be receiving her mystery message. But it should be enough to placate the anxious blonde and get her out of my office. Her wounded bird routine was starting to make me nervous. It made me feel like I'd better look out for cats.

While I whipped up a quick cover sheet and faxed the note off to Eye Candy in Vegas, Lia stood and drifted like a ghost over to the single window, peering through the blinds at the uninspiring view of dull, empty Vesper Avenue below. She stood like that while the fax machine beeped and chugged and the note fed through and spat out below. Then, when she turned back to me, I noticed that her body language had changed in some subtle way. She'd gone strangely stiff and almost formal, like some kind of catwalk Stepford wife. She turned her head on her long neck, expressionless face toward me, eyes looking at nothing.

"Where is the bathroom?" she asked.

"Back through the reception area and to the right," I told her. "Didi'll show you."

She nodded and lifted her note from the fax tray, popping the combination lock on the briefcase and opening it just enough to slip the note in. I couldn't see what else was inside and I didn't even really try all that hard to look, but I couldn't help noticing the combination for the lock. 666. Funny, I wouldn't have pegged her as a death metal fan.

I watched her slender back as she opened the door. Maybe I thought it was weird that she was carrying a man's leather briefcase instead of a purse, or maybe I was just glad to see her go. She didn't say thank you or even goodbye.

Minutes later, two men came into my office.

"You can't just walk in there," Didi was saying, but they already had.

The first guy through the door had a distinct Eastern Bloc look to his weasely, intense features. He was deeply tanned, dressed like an Armenian pop star, and had to be a good two inches shorter than me. His tall buddy in the doorway looked more like a corn-fed redneck, with thinning blond hair, cold blue eyes and a fat but powerful body like those guys that pull trucks with their teeth. His simple, all-black clothes were all business. Bad business.

"I don't book male talent," I said. "Try Eros over on Sherman Way."

"Funny," the weasely guy said. He was clearly the mouth of the two and had a faint, slightly different variation on Lia's accent. "We're looking for Lia."

"Just missed her," I told them.

"We didn't see her come out of the building," the weasel said, eyefucking me like he learned it from TV. "Why do you suppose that is?"

There was a faint shuffling from the bathroom and the weasel snapped his head toward the sound like a hungry predator.

"She had to powder her nose," he said. "Is that it?"

"Look, I don't know you or her," I said. "And I don't want anything to do with…"

Before I could finish, the redneck strode back into the reception area, past indignant Didi to the bathroom door and kicked it open.

"Hey!" Didi cried.

The bathroom was empty. Lia's expensive shoes were on the floor by the toilet. The window was open, just enough for an underfed girl to worm her way through. My office was on the second floor. It was a doable jump, though you wouldn't like hitting the concrete of the parking lot next door. Especially not with bare feet. You'd have to be pretty motivated. She obviously was.

"Listen here, you lousy sons of bitches," Didi said, fearlessly getting up in the guys' faces like an angry Jack Russell Terrier. "I don't know who the hell you think you are, but you have exactly three seconds to get the fuck out of here before I call the cops."

The men barely seemed to hear her. They just brushed her aside and left without another word.

"What the hell was that all about?" Didi has asked me.

"I have no idea," I replied, fuming at the broken lock on the bathroom door. "And frankly, I don't want to know."

Of course, at that time, I had no idea how right I was. Lying there tied to a bed with sweat all sticky and pooling on the plastic beneath me, surrounded by a variety of extremely bad men, I wanted to know even less.

4.

"Look," I said with whatever voice I could muster. "I don't know anything about any money. That girl, she just came and left when those two guys showed up. That's all I know."

"Start at the beginning," the boss said, lighting up a cigarette. "Tell me everything she told you."

"She didn't tell me anything," I said.

"She must have said something," the boss replied. "What did she want? Not work, obviously."

Why was that obvious? I had thought she was looking for work when I first saw her. I had no idea how much this asshole knew about what had happened in my office. Was he really in the dark or just looking for me to confirm his suspicions?

"She wanted to get in touch with one of my models," I told him. "Said they were friends as kids."

"She wanted to catch up?" the boss asked. "Reminisce about old times?"

I shrugged or tried to. It came out kind of funny with my arms tied out to either side.

The boss nodded, contemplating the smoke from the end of his cigarette. Then he brought the cigarette to his lips and took a deep drag. When he exhaled, two words came out with the smoke.

"Which model?"

I closed my eyes. Zandora was hardly my best friend.

She was a shallow bimbo with more designer sunglasses than sense, but she sure as hell didn't deserve to have this guy after her. The last thing I wanted to do was to drag her or anyone else into this ugly mess. I told myself to hold out, hanging on to the idea that I was protecting Zandora. I needed to at least try and be tough, because I didn't want to think of myself as the sort of person that rolled over after two punches.

"You're thinking about being brave," the boss said, taking another deep drag off his cigarette. "Don't."

"Angel, please," Sam said, his eyes bright and desperate.

"Shut up," the rhino said again and shot another curt hook at Sam's temple.

I said nothing. I squinted up at the boss and put what I hoped was a tough expression on my face. He sighed like a disappointed teacher and handed his cigarette to Jesse.

Jesse cracked a huge grin and parked the cigarette in one corner of his mouth. Then he climbed up onto the bed, straddling my hips and putting his left hand around my throat. His hands were big. I felt his thumb and forefinger pressing into the soft spots beneath my ears while the wide palm leaned down on my windpipe, cutting off my air. His face was inches from mine, pretty blue eyes gazing intently into mine like a romance novel hero as he took the cigarette from his lips with his other hand.

When I felt the heat of the cigarette moving closer to my cringing skin, all my tough-guy plans went right out the window.

"Zandora Dior," I said, my voice an airless croak.

"I'm sorry," the boss said, gesturing to Jesse to back off. "Could you repeat that?"

Jesse reluctantly let go of my neck but stayed on top of me. He was heavy. I could feel how much he was enjoying himself. I wanted to kill him.

"Zandora," I said again, only a little more clearly this time. "Zandora Dior."

"Ah," the boss said. He plucked his cigarette from between Jesse's fingers and took another drag. Jesse looked like he'd just had his favorite toy taken away.

"...but I didn't give that girl Zandora's phone number," I said. "I just told her I would give Zandora her cell number but I never did. I never did."

I could tell I'd fucked up as soon as the words were out of my mouth. The boss' eyes narrowed. Jesse's grin came back, wider than ever.

"Lia doesn't have a cell phone," the boss said.

Jesse's hand was on my throat again. He just couldn't seem to get enough of that. I know plenty of girls that are really into that asphix shit, but not me.

"Let's start again," the boss said. "From the beginning."

I won't bore you with the details, but they got it all out of me. Everything. The note, the club I faxed it to, where Zandora was staying in Vegas, everything. I would have told them about the time I took three dollars from Sister Mary Francis' desk drawer back in the second grade if they had asked. But what the boss kept coming back to I couldn't help him with. The fucker just wouldn't let go of the business with the briefcase full of money. He seemed convinced that I either had his money or knew where it was.

My lips felt hot and huge and one of my teeth felt loose in its socket. I was pretty sure my nose was broken, making it extremely difficult to breathe. My eyes were blacking up and closing down fast, blurry with blood and sweat. I was crying by then and hating myself for it. Helpless, silent tears dripped down into my ears as I turned my head to the side and spat blood onto the plastic.

"Please," I said. "Please."

Someone else had arrived, someone I could only see out of the corner of my eye, conferring with the rhino. I thought it might be the weasely guy who showed up at my office looking for Lia, but maybe not. It was difficult to concentrate with Jesse in my face, pressing down on me.

On my other side, the boss looked up and raised his eyebrows as some wordless confirmation passed between him and the rhino. He leaned in close to my ear.

"I'm going to ask you one last time," he said. He gestured to Jesse.

Jesse climbed off me, pouting like a scolded kid, and the rhino came forward, dragging Sam with him until they were both right beside the bed. I was still having trouble getting my eyes to focus, but eventually it registered that the rhino had a gun in his hand. In a weird moment of recognition, I noticed that it was the same make and model as my own, a Sig P232 that I bought after an unsettling encounter with an overzealous fan. I caught a lot of flack for choosing what several more gun-savvy friends referred to as a "girly gun." They lectured me about stopping power and how the .380 or 9mm "short" just didn't measure up to the standard 9, but I liked the way it felt in my hand better than anything else I'd tried. It looked like a toy in the rhino's thick fist. I wondered if anyone ever teased him about his choice of such a "girly gun," but all those thoughts evaporated when he raised the barrel to Sam's cheekbone.

"Jesus," Sam said, his eyes huge like a horse about to bolt. "Angel for Christ's sake, tell him!"

"Where's the money, Angel?" the boss asked.

A cold spike of adrenaline flash-froze the sick, dizzy pain in my body and I was suddenly completely sharp and lucid.

"Please," I said. "I've told you I don't know anything about your money. Why would I lie? You gotta believe me."

"You and Sam have been friends for a long time, huh?" the boss said. "He's a nice guy? A family man? You wouldn't want anything bad to happen to your old friend Sam, would you?"

I completely lost it then. I sobbed and wailed and begged like I swore I wouldn't.

The rhino shot Sam anyway, lowering the gun and putting a bullet in Sam's knee. Sam collapsed, screaming, to the floor. There is something indescribably horrible about hearing a grown man scream like that. Especially when that man is one of your oldest friends.

At that point I'm pretty sure I was screaming too. The rhino hauled Sam back up where I could see him and shoved the stubby little snout of the gun between Sam's lips.

"How about it, Angel?" the boss said.

I could not stop screaming. I wanted to lie and make up some place where the fucking imaginary money was hidden, anything to stop this madness, but it was as if the English language had deserted me. Something had snapped inside me. They had broken me and I think they knew it.

"I don't think she knows, boss," the rhino said, pulling the little gun from Sam's mouth and wiping it on Sam's shirt.

The boss nodded thoughtfully. The rhino let Sam drop back down to the floor. Jesse was back on the bed and I think he was groping me, but I barely felt it. I had stopped screaming then but I also stopped feeling anything. Call it shock or overload or whatever, my brain had decided enough was enough. It had simply put on a hat, picked up two suitcases, and fucked off to parts unknown. It wasn't that I blacked out. Everything just went distant and surreal, like something on television.

"Take care of that," the boss told the rhino, gesturing to the sobbing heap that was Sam. Then he turned back to Jesse. "She's all yours."

5.

My hot date with Jesse Black is still pretty spotty in my memory. I only remember bits and pieces. To be honest, after the hell I'd already been through, Jesse's little games barely even registered. I remember him shaking me and calling me a fucking dead fish. What the hell was he expecting? *Double Dare 2*?

While Jesse sweated and cursed and did his thing, I floated off somewhere near the ceiling. Every now and then I glanced down to see if Jesse was finished yet, but mostly I thought of Sam and Zandora and how I was going to make these fuckers pay for what they had done.

I thought Jesse was only taking a break, but then he was stuffing a rag into my mouth and duct-taping it in place. I fought to draw air through my swollen nose, sudden panic slicing through my woozy numbness. He untied me from the bed and there was a pathetic moment where I tried to make my arms and legs move, to fight him. He just smiled at the attempt, tied my hands and feet together, and lifted me in his arms. My muscles pulled and twisted the wrong way, straining against the rope, and all my bruises and cuts pulsed hot and blinding. I guess I blacked out for a minute because the next thing I knew, Jesse was dumping me gracelessly into the Civic's trunk and slamming the lid. A few minutes later, the little engine spluttered to life.

The drive seemed endless, a jerky stop-and-go nightmare of huffing fumes and banging my head every time loverboy stomped on the brakes, which seemed way more often than necessary. My entire body felt deeply bruised and full of needles and knives. My hold on consciousness was tenuous at best. I tried to hang on to random fragments of sound, a helicopter, music, a dog barking, anything that might hint at where I was being taken, but the whine of the engine swallowed everything. Or maybe it was just the nauseous buzzing in my head.

Eventually we pulled to a stop and the engine died. I heard the car door open and shut and then boots on concrete, coming around to the trunk.

I squinted up at the rectangular widescreen view as the trunk opened. Jesse was standing there, backlit by a jaundiced sodium halo. He had on a t-shirt now, black with the lurid logo of a band I'd never heard of. His face was shadowed, his posture tense and nervous. He had a gun.

There are few things more terrifying than a nervous man with a gun. He pointed it at me, then at the ground, then back at me again, wiping his lips with the knuckles of his other hand. Finally he sucked in a long breath and spoke.

"End of the line, bitch," he said.

It was clear that he had been rehearsing that snappy little piece of tough-guy dialog on the drive to wherever the hell we were. If I were directing the scene, I would have asked for another take.

He pointed the gun at me again, holding it foolishly sideways like some rap video badass. My heart felt like a trapped bird inside my chest. My bloody eyelids were swollen down to sticky slits but I wasn't going to make it easier for him by looking away or closing my eyes. If he was going to have his big gangsta moment and pop a cap in my bitch ass, it would be face to face, looking me in the eye.

In the end, it was Jesse who looked away. He turned his face to the side and squeezed his eyes shut, gun arm sticking straight out like a child about to get an injection. Then he squeezed the trigger.

The noise alone nearly gave me a heart attack. I'd always worn ear protection at the range, and although everyone knows guns are loud, you have no idea how loud they really are until someone less than six feet away is shooting at you in the trunk of a car. Ears ringing, I felt the third or fourth shot connect somewhere along the right side of my chest and under my right arm. The pain and shock of it was bright and brutal and scary as fuck. Microscopic newsboys ran through my system shouting *Extra! Extra! We've been shot!*

They always tell you not to panic, not to move if you've been shot. That you should lie still and wait for help. That getting all nuts just kills you faster. I knew that was the best thing to do, even thought it as a clear, rational sentence in my head:

Better lie still and not panic.

Of course, that only works if the person who shot you has stopped shooting.

Jesse was still randomly filling the trunk with lead, firing blindly in my general direction. I felt another bullet clip my thigh like a lash from a single-tail whip.

My body duly noted my brain's helpful suggestion about staying calm and then proceeded to flip completely out. I must have bumped my head flinching and flailing around or maybe I just passed out from pain or shock because the next thing I remembered was coming to in the dark trunk and fighting to piece it all back together and remember where the hell I was. That's where you came in.

6.

So once I figured out I was in the trunk of a car, I remembered the blue Civic and from there it was a swift re-connect the dots back to Jesse and Sam and the girl with the briefcase.

I also remembered that I had been shot, or thought I had. It obviously hadn't been by a very good shot, since I was still around to worry about it, but it did seem fairly pressing that I get some sort of medical attention. I felt like someone was digging a fork around in my right side just below the armpit and it hurt like hell if I took a deep breath. I thought maybe my right arm was also hit, as there was a hot nasty pain on the soft underside of my triceps. Moving my right hand made the pain in my arm crank up from ugly to excruciating so I yanked and twisted my left again and again until I was able to work the knots loose around my wrists. It was fairly easy. Jesse was a lousy rigger.

Once I had my hands loose, I was able to rip the tape off my mouth. I spat out the crumpled rag and the meager contents of my stomach immediately followed. It was mostly sour old blood. I managed not to get too much on myself, which was pretty impressive in such a small space.

When I was able, I used my awkward left hand to free my ankles. My feet were icy numb and howled with sharp needling pain as the blood started to flow back in. You'd think there'd be a point where so much of your body hurt so badly that it would hang a sign on the door saying NO VACANCY and refuse to accept any new pain. Apparently not.

Free now but still stuck in the puke-stinking trunk, I needed to figure a way out. The Civic had been built before anyone thought to put safety latches on the insides of trunks. The only way out would be by kicking down the folding back seats. I had a long discussion with my legs about the idea of kicking anything. At first they were having none of it, but once I explained how difficult it would be for them if my heart stopped beating or severe blood loss eventually caused the cessation of all brain function, they reluctantly agreed to do their part, though not without a lot of surly grumbling.

For a piece of shit, the latches on the Civic's back seats were annoyingly well made and solid. I had to brace my back against the rear of the trunk and push with all the strength left in my legs. The strain of it made my head fill with dizzy red spangles, but eventually the seat on the passenger side flopped down, letting a weak wash of yellow light into my dark little world. It hurt my eyes and made me feel like a Morlock as I wiggled out through the gap.

Now that I could see where I was, I still had no idea where I was. Rundown industrial wasteland like this was all over Southern California. All over the country, even, but the drive had felt like less than thirty minutes so I figured I must still be in or near the L.A. area.

The Civic turned out to be parked at the far end of a lot behind a large empty warehouse with mostly broken windows. I thought I heard a train somewhere close, but couldn't see any tracks. The sodium lights illuminating the scene sat atop graffitied poles around the warehouse next door, which was apparently still in use. On the other side was a weedy vacant lot.

I had been so focused on the series of tasks required to get myself out of the trunk that I had almost lost track of the bigger picture. Now that I was loose and alive, the cold fury that had taken second place to basic survival suddenly moved up to center stage. I was so angry, it felt almost like love. Angry for being made to feel helpless and scared. Angry for having my nice comfortable life torn open and savaged and left bleeding. Angry for getting the shit kicked out of me and Sam too, all for something I didn't even understand. I knew what I wanted to do. I wanted to find Jesse and the rhino and their boss, that fucker with the bland everyman face. Find them and kill them.

I slowly pushed open the Civic's passenger-side door and put my bare feet on the grimy concrete, high on beautiful, full-color action movie fantasies of dishing out .44-caliber vigilante justice. That's when I realized I was naked.

I'm about as far from shy as you can get, but walking around a neighborhood like this in the altogether was the dictionary definition of a bad idea. I figured I needed to table the whole vendetta thing until I could find something to cover my girly bits.

There was nothing in the car at all, not even a map or an old burger wrapper. I thought about trying to tear the vinyl off the seats but it was too tough and my right arm was throbbing and I just wanted to get the hell out of there. I scanned the narrow lot, searching for anything that I could use to cover myself. Nothing but a single torn black trash bag, more than half full of stuff I didn't even want to think about. I shook out the contents onto the cement and turned the bag inside out so that the wet side would not touch my skin. The smell was appalling. I tore open the bottom all the way until I had a sort of skirt-shaped thing and stepped squeamishly into it. Instead of tying it at my waist, I pulled it up to just above my breasts, like a towel. The bottom of the bag covered the cheeks of my ass but only if I stood completely straight. It was bad, barely better than naked and much, much stinkier. Breathing shallowly though my mouth, I limped around to the front of the warehouse.

The faded sign on the building's rough brick hide gave away nothing. HW Equipment Ltd. I saw an address spray painted above a heavily barred door. 23202. No street name.

The warehouse was near the dead end of a desolate block of ugly industrial buildings. It felt like a marathon just to make it to a cross street. When I finally found one, my eyes had trouble focusing on the signs. East 37th and Saco Street. I didn't recognize either one. I could have been anywhere.

I found a rusty shopping cart at the intersection. It was full of swollen, moldy phonebooks and an eclectic collection of glass jars containing, apparently, urine. There didn't seem to be an owner nearby. In fact, there were no humans anywhere that I could see. No homeless, no hookers, no junkies, not even cars. Nothing, like I was the last girl on earth and had somehow missed out on the apocalypse while I was in the trunk. There was, however, a shirt in the shopping cart. It was plaid, stiff, and only slightly less repugnant than the garbage bag, but I was thrilled to have it. I slipped my arms into the ragged sleeves and pulled the trash bag down to form a longer skirt. Now if only I could find some shoes, I'd be set.

I impulsively decided to take the shopping cart. It helped tremendously to lean my battered bones on the handle as I limped along the empty street. Plus, if I actually did encounter a fellow human, shopping carts are the world's best urban camouflage. They have the power to make a person invisible in any big city in America. You hear a shopping cart coming down the street, you immediately look away from the person pushing it. *Homeless,* you tell yourself. *Better not look, or they'll ask for money.*

I thought I might really die before I found a phone. More and more it seemed like the best course of action would be to just lie down on the pavement. The only thing that kept me going was picturing Jesse Black's cocky smirk disintegrating under a point-blank lead facial.

I finally saw a sign for a tiny Mexican *mercado* at the far end of the street. The *mercado* was closed, but there was a payphone out front, plastered with stickers advertising taxis, escorts and phone cards with special rates to Central and South America. Amazingly, the phone worked.

I punched 9-1-1 on the grimy keypad. A woman came on the line, asking about the nature of my emergency. I told her I had been shot and gave the address of the *mercado*. She told me to hold on, that help was on the way.

Hearing this, my body wanted to pass back out. Mission accomplished, right? Time to lie down and wait for the cavalry. But my mind wouldn't shut up about what had happened, fighting to make logic out of the madness. I thought of feisty little Didi giving those goons what for in my office and was suddenly very afraid for her. I had to make sure she was okay.

Even though I have a great memory for numbers and addresses, it took me a minute to pull my own calling card number out of the numb mush of my brain. As soon as I did, I phoned Didi's home and her cell. Nothing. That scared me even worse, since I knew Didi to answer the phone any time, day or night. Even on the toilet or in the heat of her frequent intimate liaisons. And no, I didn't want to leave a message. What I had to say was for her ears only. Paranoia coiled around my aching ribs, making it even harder to breathe. No sign of an ambulance. I couldn't stand the thought of anything happening to Didi. I needed to call someone to go check up on her, to make sure she was okay. There was only one person I could think of who would be awake, willing and able. I called Malloy.

Lalo Malloy was the new guy, since Daring Angels' faithful security escort Joe Saturnino got married and moved to Florida. I always employ a guy part-time to drive my girls to gigs with new production companies and hang out while they shoot. I like an older guy, reliable and mature enough not to go all gaga over the girls, but still intimidating enough to make sure no one thinks to try anything funny with my models. I pay a small hourly wage and the girls top it off with tips. Not bad for a part-time gig.

Malloy was an ex-cop like Joe, though he looked much more like a thug. Six-two, thick through the shoulders and the middle and pretty much everywhere else. Olive drab eyes that sized up the world through a taciturn tough-guy squint. Buzz-cut hair gone solid silver and under it a face like a police sketch based on the descriptions of terrorized victims. His left ear was slightly cauliflowered, just enough to let you know that he was no stranger to knuckles. His look was perfect for the job and he came highly recommended by Joe. They had been buddies back in the old LAPD days and had both left the force under less than sterling circumstances. I didn't ask and they didn't tell.

"Lalo's okay," Joe told me with a smirk the day he introduced us, faking a punch to Malloy's meaty shoulder. "For a Hispamick."

"A what?" I had asked.

"His daddy was Irish," Joe explained. "And mama's Mexican. A Hispamick."

Malloy himself seemed neither amused nor annoyed by the joke. He just shrugged and put his big hands in his pockets.

He'd been driving my girls for almost two months and I still didn't really know him all that well. He wasn't an easy guy to get to know. Came in, did his job and left. Solid, but not much for casual conversation. I felt really strange calling him in the middle of the night like this, but there just wasn't anyone else. It took me several wrong numbers to get him on the line. He picked up on the first ring.

"Malloy," he said, like he was still answering the phone at the Homicide desk.

I had no idea what the hell I was going to say to him.

"Malloy," I repeated, feeling like I had forgotten how to speak. "It's…I…"

"I'll call you back," he said suddenly and hung up.

Baffled, I stared at the dirty blue receiver in my hand, then slowly put it back on the cradle. I leaned over the handle of the shopping cart and maybe grayed out for a little while, but then the phone rang, scaring me and making me jump. It hurt.

"Malloy?" I said into the phone.

"Angel," he replied. I could hear traffic in the background. I figured he must have gotten the number off caller ID and then gone out to a payphone. "You wanna tell me what the hell is going on?"

I felt suddenly sure I really was going to black out. What the hell *was* going on? I didn't even know where to begin.

"Angel," Malloy was saying. "Angel, are you there?"

I tried to tell Malloy about the blonde and the briefcase full of money and Jesse and the blue Civic. I can't imagine I made much sense, but eventually Malloy got the gist of it.

"Did you call an ambulance?" he asked.

It took me a minute to answer that. Did I call an ambulance? Things were getting woozy and confusing and I just wanted to lie down.

"Yeah," I eventually said, or must have because then Malloy was telling me to get the hell away from the *mercado*, to hide from the ambulance.

"Hide from the ambulance?" I said. Nothing seemed to make any sense. "But why…"

"Angel," Malloy said. "If you let them take you to the hospital, you're going to be arrested for the murder of Sam Hammer."

7.

"Angel," Malloy was saying again. "Angel."

His voice sounded so far away that I thought I was still on the phone until I felt his hands on me, wrapping a rough blanket around my body and lifting me like a tired kid. I have no idea how I got away from the phone and the *mercado* but I did. I also had no idea how Malloy found me, but he did. I've never been so happy to see anyone in my life. I would have kissed him if my lips hadn't felt like I'd just kissed a belt sander. He bundled me into the passenger seat of his blocky old SUV.

Things went all non-sequential and confusing again. The next thing that seemed solid was me in a doctor's office. I was lying on one of those examination tables with the paper that rolls down to cover it fresh for each patient. There were stirrups, like at the gynecologist. My trash bag dress was gone and I was wearing one of those backless deals they give you in the hospital. I seemed relatively clean and odor-free, but the cacophony of pain made it hard to concentrate.

I rolled on my side, briefly breathless from the effort. That's when I noticed a tan leather locking restraint hanging from the nearest stirrup. I frowned and looked around.

There were three other restraints hanging from the table, plus a thick leather strap that presumably buckled around the waist. Beside the table was a stainless steel tray on wheels, filled with terrifying antique medical instruments. There was a red rubber enema bag on a pole by my head. The glass-front cabinet against the opposite wall was filled with boxes of needles and bags of saline solution and clear plastic speculums and catheter kits and medical staplers. Above the examination table was a large framed photograph of an icy blonde in skin-tight white latex. Her waist was corseted down to insect proportions and her long legs were laced into thigh-high boots. She held a hypodermic needle the size of a .357 Magnum.

I struggled to sit up, dizzy and sick but then Malloy was there and so was the blonde, although she was dressed down in faded jeans and a white t-shirt. Her pale, shiny face was free of make up. She was still stunning.

"Angel," Malloy said. "Lie down, will you?"

"Where the hell am I?" I asked. "This isn't a hospital."

The blonde smiled. Malloy shook his head.

"It was this or Tijuana," he said.

I didn't want to lie down but my body overrode my brain and I fell back on the table. I looked up at the photo.

"You brought me to a *dominatrix*?" I asked, pressing my thumb and forefinger into the corners of my eyes and then flinching at how much that hurt.

"This is Ulka," Malloy said. "She's gonna fix you up."

"You've gotta be kidding," I said.

"Don't be afraid," the blonde said in a clipped German accent that did nothing to reassure me. "I am very good. And much cleaner than Tijuana."

She turned and began washing her hands at a steel sink with foot-operated faucets. Suddenly I remembered

Didi, how she hadn't answered her phone. I'd meant to ask Malloy to check on Didi, not rescue my sorry ass.

"Shit!" I said, sitting up too fast and feeling stabbed by a dozen knives, the largest just beneath my armpit. "Malloy, I need you to go check on Didi right away."

"Keep your shirt on," Malloy told me. "I talked to Didi on the way to pick you up. She's ticked off at the cops who took her in for questioning and worried sick about you, but otherwise she's fine."

Relief stole the very last drops of energy I had left. My body slumped back down on the table while my brain concentrated on not puking. It worked, but just barely.

"I'm ready," Ulka said.

"I'll wait outside," Malloy replied.

I wanted to ask him to stay with me, but I felt suddenly shy and embarrassed and then it was too late, because he was gone, leaving me alone with Ulka, She Wolf of the SS.

I've never gotten along all that well with pro Dommes. The ones I've made videos with always seemed to look down on me and my girls because we do things on camera that they feel are beneath them. The way I see it, we're all in the same business. Providing visual stimulation. Does it really make a difference if that stimulation is the most exotic, esoteric fetish or just good old fashioned baby-making? Bottom line: Everyone is doing the same thing while they watch it.

"I'm afraid I don't have any sort of anesthesia," Ulka said, slipping her mannish hands into latex gloves. "That would be sort of counterproductive in my line of work."

"Great," I said, looking away toward the wall.

"I do have some of these," she said, pressing several chalky white pills into my palm. "You'll need them."

I didn't even ask what they were. I just dry swallowed them all before she could even bring a paper cup of water to my lips.

I waited impatiently for the pills to work while she started to examine the mess below my right armpit. Her hands were much more gentle than I would have expected.

"It looks like the bullet went right between your arm and your torso," she said. "Maybe bounced off a rib and then angled through the triceps. Either you are very lucky or the person who shot you is very stupid."

"A little of both, I think," I replied.

"You will need a few stitches," she said.

"Stitches?" I felt suddenly lightheaded. "Can you do that?"

"Of course," she said, selecting a sterilized paper packet the size of an index card from a box in the cabinet. "Sutures are my specialty, though to tell the truth, my clients rarely actually need them."

I wouldn't say that she was nice, but she had a wry, deadpan sense of humor and her hands were steady as stone. Of course it hurt like hell, but she didn't make me feel like a slut. She treated me almost like a real patient. I've had legit doctors treat me worse. I wound up liking her far more than I had planned to.

"How do you know Malloy?" I asked between bouts of silent, jaw grinding pain. "He's not a client, is he?"

I couldn't see Malloy crawling around on the floor begging to lick a woman's boots, but you never knew these days. Ulka smirked and shook her head as she snipped the thread from the last stitch.

"Nothing like that," she said. "He provides security

for me when I book night sessions with new clients. I removed a bullet from his right thigh two years ago. That was amazing. Well, for me anyway." She placed a bandage over her handiwork. "One more thing."

Before I could protest or even register what was happening, she was pressing her large thumbs against the mess of my nose, giving the whole thing a decisive shove to the left. The pain was indescribable.

"You're done," she said, slapping a piece of tape over the bridge of my nose.

Truer words were never spoken. There was no need to stick a fork in me. The pills had kicked in with a vengeance while I wasn't paying attention and now that the bright foreground pain of the stitches and whatever the fuck she'd done to my nose was over, I could feel everything shutting down. I was most definitely, unequivocally done. I vaguely remember Malloy returning to carry me somewhere and cold leather against my bruised skin and then merciful nothing.

8.

I didn't exactly wake up. It was more like I fought my way up through a twilight sea of gauzy pain and confusion for what felt like centuries until I finally focused on Malloy's profile and the glowing tip of his cigarette.

"You're awake," he said. Not a question, just a statement.

"If you want to call it that," I replied. My throat hurt. Come to think of it, everything hurt.

I looked around and saw that I was in a small lounge that could have been the chic waiting room for a celebrity plastic surgeon. Malloy pushed an oversized white mug of coffee across the table till it was close enough for me to reach.

"You wanna go first," he asked. "Or should I?"

I looked down at the coffee and then back at Malloy. He must have been up all night but didn't look it. He looked the same as ever, unchanging as a stone idol, except he had on a different cheap suit jacket, dark gray instead of dark green. I'd probably bled on him at some point the night before.

I picked up the coffee with my left hand. It smelled wonderful, but my stomach wasn't too sure about the prospect. I took a sip anyway. I needed it.

I was mildly surprised by the fact that the coffee was exactly the way I like it. Black with one Sweet'N Low. Funny, since I didn't recall ever telling Malloy how I take my coffee.

"You go first," I finally managed to say. My throat hurt worse than the day I shot *Sword Swallowers 14* with Axl Rodd and Dix Steele. My voice sounded thick and gritty, like somebody else.

"Uniform patrol found Sam Hammer's body in your abandoned car over by the Van Nuys airport," Malloy said, stubbing his cigarette in a smooth stone ashtray. "One in the knee and two to the back of the head. Tortured and then executed. Stone cold. They're considering the possibility of a male accomplice but it sounds as if they like you for the shooter."

I didn't do a spit take with the coffee, but I came close. The idea that Sam was dead was bad enough but the fact that the cops thought I'd done it was even more unreal.

"Why me?" I asked, forcing the words through numb lips. "Why would they..."

"You own a Sig P232?"

I felt a sick, spiraling feeling of hopelessness and despair gathering under my solar plexus. Now I knew why a big butch bastard like that fucking rhino would use such a girly gun. Because it *was* a girl's gun. Mine.

"Fuck," I said softly.

I remembered that bland-faced motherfucker telling me he had my house and office searched, looking for his goddamn money. Whoever did the search—maybe that weasely Eastern Bloc guy—must have stolen my gun from my nightstand drawer and brought it to the house in Bel Air. I was starting to grasp just how meticulously and thoroughly I had been fucked.

"They found your Sig in a dumpster around the corner from the abandoned vehicle," Malloy said. "A coupla young hard-ons from the Valley division questioned me just before you called. Thought maybe I might be the male accomplice." He shook his head. "I'm ironclad. I was out propping up an old buddy in the department, a detective sergeant going through a nasty divorce."

"I…" I tried to swallow, but my throat felt squeezed down to nothing. "I didn't kill Sam, I swear. You don't believe this bullshit, do you? If I was going to kill Sam, you think I'd be stupid enough to shoot him with my own legally registered gun and then just leave his body sitting in my fucking car?"

Malloy looked at me with his narrow alligator eyes, wordlessly sizing me up. An endless minute passed. He pulled another cigarette from a crumpled pack, then offered the pack to me. I shook my head. He shrugged and put the pack away, then stuck the cigarette between his lips.

"No," he finally said, shaking his head as he lit up with a battered Zippo. "I don't buy it. Smells like setup city, but it's not just that." He snapped the lighter shut. "I could maybe buy you getting all pissed off and blowing some guy away in the heat of the moment. But the truth is, you just don't strike me as the type who'd torture a good friend and then finish him with a cold-blooded, professional execution. No offense, but I just don't think you've got it in you for that kind of action. You want to tell me what really happened?"

Malloy was completely still and silent as I filled him in. His cigarette burned unsmoked between two thick fingers. It was disconcerting. You don't realize how much you depend on a listener to spur your story on with little nods and noises and various cues to continue like "Really?" or "No shit." However, I did get the feeling that

I was being listened to more intently than ever before. Like I was feeding information into a machine for processing. I told him everything, starting from the blonde with the briefcase and ending with him showing up to scrape my ass off the sidewalk.

When I was done, I sipped more coffee, just to have something to do with my shaking hands. He took a deep drag off the cigarette and then flicked the long ash into the stone ashtray.

"You want my help," he said. Again a statement, not a question.

"Yeah," I replied. "I want you to help me find the fuckers who did this to me. I can pay you."

He shook his head.

"Your bank accounts'll be frozen by now."

"I have money," I said. "Cash. In my line of business, it never hurts to have a safety net."

He arched a silver brow and then killed the cigarette.

"Keep it," he replied. "You're gonna need it."

"Does that mean you won't help me?" I asked.

He shrugged. There was a long moment of awkward silence. I'd done all the begging I was going to do the night before, so I just kept my mouth shut and waited for his answer.

"I'll do what I can," he said eventually.

I wanted to hug him, but my ribs hurt and he didn't seem like the hugging type.

"Thanks," I said instead.

"Right," he said. "I guess I'd better get on the road." He looked at his ugly watch. "If I leave now, I should be able to make Vegas by noon."

I frowned and it hurt the bruised skin above my eyes.

"What do you mean *I*?" I asked. "It's *we*. You can't leave me here. Wherever you're going, I'm going with you."

"No," he said with a terse shake of his head. "You're gonna stay here where it's safe."

"I'm not some helpless princess, you know," I said. "I can take care of myself."

He looked up at me and the ghost of a smirk haunted one corner of his thin lips.

"I can see that," he replied.

"Fuck you!" I spat, but my mad face wouldn't stay on. I snorted through my swollen nose. "You should see the other guy."

His tiny smirk swelled into an expression that could almost be mistaken for a smile.

"All right, boss," he said. "I guess we better get you something to wear."

The room Malloy ushered me into had a gold sign on the door.

"*Sissy Boudoir*," I read out loud. "I think I did a girl/girl scene with her back in '94."

Again, that little twitch of a smile, quick as an insect wing at the corner of Malloy's mouth, as he chivalrously held the door open for me.

The "Sissy Boudoir" was dimly lit and tricked out with pink satin and red velvet. No angles. Everything was soft and rounded in a way that made it feel sort of like being inside a huge plush vagina. To the left was a walk-in closet filled with extra-large feminine attire. Boat-sized pumps with ten-inch heels. Trampy stripper dresses and frilly French maid costumes that would have fit Malloy. Full-figured bras, enormous lace panties and boxes of queen-sized pantyhose. I was about to make some kind of snide comment when I caught a glimpse of my own reflection in the full-length mirror.

I wasn't ready for that, but I don't know how you could be. When my eyes first snagged on the pale figure in the hospital gown, I was startled because I thought it was someone else. When I realized it was me, I felt dizzy, stricken with a kind of horrified disbelief.

"Jesus," I whispered, pressing a palm to the cool surface of the mirror.

My face was a lurid Halloween mask, haphazardly painted in every shade of bruise. My proud Italian nose was massively swollen and lumpy under a stripe of clean white tape. Both my eyes were black, the right more than the left, making me look like an asymmetrical purple panda. My lower lip was twice the size of the upper and had a thick, crusty split down the middle. My forehead was studded with contusions, giving me a heavy, Neanderthal brow. There was blood crusted in my hair.

My arms and legs were also covered with bruises and scrapes and I could see the bristly blue stitches protruding like bug legs from my right side just under the armpit. But my gaze kept returning to that face that couldn't possibly be my face. I suddenly understood why Savannah had shot herself after she'd bashed up her face in that car accident. Not sixteen hours ago, I had been staring into a mirror and fretting about crow's feet and less than perfectly perky breasts. I had to laugh or I'd start screaming.

"Sure, it's ugly today," Malloy said, pulling a dress off its hanger and handing it to me. "But it'll be better in a week and back to normal in two. You might want to get some work on that nose when this is all over."

I couldn't even imagine what "all over" really meant. What my life would be like when and if this was all over. Or what it was going to take to make it that way.

Instead of dwelling on the uncertain future, I forced myself to concentrate on the little tasks in front of me right now. Tasks like shedding the hospital gown and slipping into the dress while Malloy graciously looked away, as if the whole world hadn't already seen me naked a million times. The dress was the smallest of the lot but still fit me like a laundry bag. It was black and probably would have looked much sluttier if it actually fit. There were no bras in anything close to my size and the dress' deep sweetheart neckline hung droopy and unflattering on my bruised chest. Malloy had to help me zip the thing and when I looked back in the mirror I suddenly felt like crying. I wanted desperately to go home, take a shower in my safe green bathroom, and change into my own comfortable clothes. I wanted a bra that looked nice. My favorite boots. I wanted to open my neatly organized, sweet-smelling underwear drawer and pick out a nice clean cotton thong. The thought of my little house and all my books and clothes and personal things barricaded behind yellow tape and rifled by smirking cops fed my helpless anger and heated my tears to near boiling as I fought to hold them back. I turned away from the mirror and that horrible ugly face and started randomly flinging shoes around, searching for anything that was less than three sizes too big.

"I can't," I said. "These are all fucking huge." I picked up a pair of cherry-red patent leather pumps. "Eleven!" I shouted, tossing them aside. "Thirteen!" I read off the print on a pair of clear plastic platforms. "*Fuck!*"

I flailed out with my left arm and knocked over a wire shoe rack. Huddled and shaking in a pile of trashy drag shoes, I couldn't fight the tears anymore.

Who did I think I was kidding? I wasn't some kind of badass action movie heroine. I was just a beat-up barefoot dead girl with no house and no business and no chance in hell of doing anything but getting my dumb ass killed for real. I might as well just turn myself in. At least in jail, I'd get shoes that fit.

Malloy turned politely away from my tears just like he had looked away while I was changing. He stood like that for a minute, giving me space to have my girly breakdown, then spoke.

"Tell you what," he said softly. "I'll carry you barefoot to my car and then we can swing by Payless or something. You're a seven, right?"

"Right," I said, snuffling back tearsnot and pushing my hair back from my face. "Seven."

It's funny, but that was exactly what I needed to break me out of my little pity-party. I normally hated that Men-Are-From-Mars, testosterone-driven impulse boys get where they want to solve all my problems by troubleshooting me like buggy software and offering up a simple concrete solution to stop my tears. But if Malloy had done something more intuitive and nurturing like hugging me or telling me everything was going to be all right, I would have disintegrated into a useless puddle. His simple answer to the problem of the big shoes gave me something to hold on to. Payless. Right. Good idea. It allowed me to pretend that the lack of shoes that fit really was the reason I was crying.

9.

We wound up at Target instead of Payless. I waited in the car with my knees tucked up under my chin while Malloy went in. I watched normal people going in and out with kids and bags, all living normal lives in which nobody had ever really hurt them. I hated them for being so clueless, like I used to be.

When Malloy came out he had twice as many shopping bags as I'd expected. When I looked at what he'd bought, I felt the same sort of baffled wonder I had experienced over the morning coffee.

The first shopping bag he handed me contained items that were plainer and cheaper, but otherwise identical to the outfit I had been wearing the last time I saw him, a pair of low-rise jeans and a black tank top. But instead of the high-heeled boots I had been wearing that day, he'd bought me a pair of sleek black athletic shoes. He'd also included a utilitarian black fleece hoodie, since it was October and the weather was drifting toward cool at night. Another smaller bag contained two black thongs, a black bra and a package of black cotton socks. The bra was the correct size, but Malloy had chosen a more modest, unpadded style, rather than my usual cleavage enhancing push-up in-your-face variety. It didn't matter. I was amazed by his flawless memory for detail. The sizes were all perfect. I didn't think the last six men who'd actually touched my breasts could have guessed my bra size at gunpoint, but this man I barely knew remembered how I took my coffee and the exact style of jeans I like. I snuck a glance over at Malloy as he handed me a bag of travel-sized toiletries. He looked the same, deadpan and squinting against the morning sun as he lit another cigarette. I wondered if maybe I was starting to develop a bit of a crush on him. Or maybe it was just some dumb girly thing about being rescued. Either way, I found myself suddenly speculating about what it might be like with him. I wondered if he would crack open and get wild in the sack, or if he would do the deed with the same quiet determination as everything else he did.

I think he might have sensed my impure thoughts, but if he did, he chose not to comment. He just fished a pair of black sunglasses out of one of the bags, tore off the tag and told me to put them on. I felt suddenly embarrassed, hyperaware of my ugly, beat-up face and dumpy dress.

"Thanks," I said quietly, slipping on the sunglasses.

"You're welcome," he replied and pulled out of the lot.

Malloy wanted to rent a car, something generic and forgettable, just to be on the safe side. He transferred all the shopping bags and a roomy green gym bag from his own SUV into the little rented Kia Rio. Then as soon as we were out of the rental place, Malloy pulled into a big supermarket parking lot and swiftly snagged the license plates off a crappy little Honda not unlike my hated Civic, stashing the Kia's legit plates in the gym bag. I thought he was being kind of paranoid, but of course it turned out he was right.

On our way out of town, we stopped at a 7-Eleven. I changed in the bathroom and stuffed the hateful tranny dress into the trash bin. I brushed the sticky tangles from my hair and the funk from my teeth and then splashed some cold water on my swollen face. That hurt like hell but I felt better once it had been done.

A chubby blonde teenage girl with giant hoop earrings and too much lip gloss pushed open the bathroom door and then froze when she saw me at the sinks.

"Oh," she said, tucking her pink face down like she'd been smacked. "Sorry."

She turned and left without meeting my eyes. Like she had caught me fingering myself or shooting up. The bathroom had several stalls and was meant to accommodate more than one person, yet she fled the moment she saw me. I looked up into the spotted mirror at my face. I couldn't really blame her. I put my sunglasses back on.

When I left the bathroom, I deliberately dawdled in the store, watching the reactions of the people around me. It was amazing. Once they noticed the bruises, they looked away like I was a leper. Men would scope my ass in the new jeans, but when their gaze hit my face their smirks would evaporate and they would suddenly notice some really fascinating nutritional information on the label of their Red Bull can. Women would cringe from my bruises like they were contagious, like looking at me would remind them that they weren't really safe after all. No one wanted to see me, to think about what might have happened to me, and so they did everything in their power to unsee me. I had a sudden perverse urge to shake people and force them to look but it occurred to me that my new Teflon face was probably a good thing. After all, a murder suspect on the lam doesn't want to be looked at.

I imagined a tan, handsome cop with a thick mustache questioning the girl with the big earrings.

"Can you describe the individual you encountered in the restroom?" he would ask.

"She was all beat up," the girl would answer.

"What color was her hair?" he would ask.

The girl would chew her gooey lower lip and shrug.

"How about her eyes?"

"Black," the girl would say.

As I hustled back to the rented car, I wondered briefly if people thought that Malloy was the one who did this to me.

The Silver Spur Motel in Vegas was just what you'd expect. Squeezed in between a gas station and a modest storefront that housed a different fly-by-night business every week, it was a blocky stucco U curled around a narrow parking lot. Cheap and tawdry but still clean and relatively safe, not too scary for a beautiful young woman traveling alone with a large roll of small bills. It was far from the flashy neon circus of the Strip but conveniently located within spitting distance of several of the biggest titty bars in Vegas. All the girls stayed there when they were dancing at Eye Candy or Cheetah's or Sin. I must have stayed there myself a hundred times. It was almost like a dorm for road girls and feature dancers, except there was no watchful dorm mother to keep out gentleman callers. Just a silent, thousand-year-old Indian desk clerk who made an art out of looking the other way. As a result, there was tons of action at the Spur, both professional and recreational. The girls called it the Silver Sperm.

When I spotted the familiar cowboy boot-shaped sign, I told Malloy to make a left into the lot. It was early still, just before 1PM. We saw a pair of hung-over afternoon-shift girls, bottle blondes in velour track suits lugging knock-off Louis Vuitton gig bags, but the place was otherwise pretty dead. Most of the night-shift girls would not even be awake for another hour or two. Malloy clocked the busty blondes as dispassionately as he took note of the other cars in the lot. I spotted Zandora's Lexus parked right by the office and directed Malloy to park beside it. He shook his head and parked further back instead, as far away from the street and the girls as he could get.

"Put your sweatshirt on," he said as we waited for the two girls to load their things into their rental car and pull out of the lot. "And put the hood up. Here."

He handed me a pair of latex gloves. I watched him as he stretched a second pair over his own broad hands.

"Are you serious?" I asked, frowning down at the gloves.

He didn't answer. He didn't have to. Clearly he was. I put the gloves on.

Zandora was in room 202, upstairs on the second level. As I stood before the plain white door with its shiny silver number, I had a sick, visceral flashback of screaming that number at the top of my lungs. I shuddered and Malloy put a heavy, gloved paw on my shoulder.

There was a sudden frantic scuffle and thump behind the door, followed by a high-pitched man's voice cursing loudly in what had to be Romanian. Then, a louder thump and Zandora's voice shouting something that sounded sort of like "pizza man." Apparently the guy didn't like being called a pizza man, because what I heard next could only be fists on soft flesh.

"Jesus," I said, belly twisted tight as my heart fluttered high in my throat.

"You up for this?" Malloy asked, reaching beneath his jacket to unsnap a shoulder holster I hadn't even noticed until just then.

Was I?

Before I could answer, he kicked open the cheap lock and moved into the shadowy room, gun out and covering the space inside with smooth, professional ease. Cattle-prodded by adrenaline, I followed Malloy, feeling like an understudy with no time to rehearse.

My old pal was inside, that sawed-off, weasely Eastern Bloc guy that had been looking for Lia. He was crouching over a crumpled, fetal Zandora and shaking out his right hand like it hurt. His surprised face was turned up toward Malloy, eyes wide.

"Who the hell are you?" he asked.

"Get up," Malloy replied, making a terse upward gesture with the barrel of his gun.

My eyes were scanning the shadows for the weasel's buddy, that big blond redneck that had backed him up that day in my office. Before I could remember how to make my voice work and warn Malloy, the door slammed back into Malloy's shoulder and the redneck was on him, gripping Malloy's gun hand by the wrist. Together, they stumble-waltzed in a tight circle, slamming the door closed, knocking over a chair and bumping a tiny table to the right of the door. A flimsy pink and silver gown that Zandora had been ironing on a hotel towel fluttered to the floor at their feet. The iron followed, hissing and dribbling hot water on the carpet.

After a fierce struggle, the pistol flew from Malloy's hand. The redneck broke loose and made an awkward sideways lunge for the gun. With a frightening economy of movement, Malloy smashed the little table with his right foot, ripped loose one of its metal legs, and spun around to crack the redneck in the temple. Malloy followed up with a swift kick and the redneck went down on his side in a crumpled, bleeding heap.

Before I could blink, Malloy had the gun again and was pointing it at the weasely guy straddling Zandora.

"Get off her and get your fucking hands up," Malloy said. "Angel, get his gun."

Recognition blossomed in the guy's narrow eyes as he raised himself slowly to his feet, bloody palms framing his disbelieving face.

It seemed to take centuries for me to figure out how to peel myself off the wall and make my arms and legs obey my brain. I put on the toughest face I could muster, walked over to the weasel and forced myself to start feeling around under his obnoxious silk shirt. It was bright canary yellow with a jaunty, Vegas-themed pattern of playing cards and dice, made even more lurid by the recent addition of wet crimson splatters. I could smell his armpits and his hot, minty breath and his eyes kept darting between me and Malloy as I patted his wiry body down. My hands felt clumsy under the latex gloves. Someone with a clue probably would have found the compact .38 in the small of his back right away. I found it eventually and gingerly tweezed it between my thumb and forefinger like something nasty.

"Got it," I said.

The weasel muttered while I backed away and tried to make my numb fingers hold the unfamiliar gun the way my firearms safety instructor had taught me.

"Over there," Malloy told the weasel, gesturing with his gun toward the bathroom door.

"You're dead," the weasel spat, showing me his long yellow teeth like a dog. "Dead."

"Shut up," Malloy said.

"You too, big man," he told Malloy. "You and this whore."

I somehow managed to thumb off the safety, aiming low.

"Fuck you," I said.

The weasel's eyes cut over to his fallen comrade and widened slightly. Malloy frowned and turned back to the redneck just in time to dodge the airborne iron as it flew into the mirrored closet door, shattering the glass. The redneck barreled into Malloy, wrapping thick sunburned arms around Malloy's chest. As they grappled and grunted, the weasel started inching closer to me.

"Stay back, fuckhead!" I said, hating the pinched, girly squeak in my voice.

"You gonna shoot me?" he asked, arching an eyebrow and sliding closer.

"I said stay back!"

"What if I don't?" he asked.

There was a furious howl and my gaze flicked over toward Malloy. He had two fingers of his right hand digging into the corner of the redneck's mouth, stretching the guy's cheek out from his teeth in a painful imitation of a kid pulling a funny face.

Not a second later, the weasel was on me, slamming my head against the wall and groping for the gun. I wrenched my hand free from his grip and slammed the gun down into his leering face. He staggered back and Malloy looked over. The weasel locked eyes with Malloy. Malloy had a smear of crimson on his cheek and his eyes had gone dark and cold. The redneck was struggling in his arms. Malloy slammed a fist into his throat, hard, without breaking eye contact with the weasel. The redneck stopped struggling.

The weasel turned, tore open the door and ran.

"Shit," Malloy said. He let the redneck drop and took off after the weasel. "Wait here," he called from outside.

Then he was gone and I was alone in a wrecked motel room with a dying friend and a dying scumbag.

The redneck's breath was coming in ragged, wet-sounding bursts. Malloy had punched him repeatedly in the throat, and I could tell he was choking. I tried not to look at his bruised and broken face. It looked way too much like mine.

I turned my attention to Zandora instead. She lay where the weasel had left her, curled small and barely breathing in front of the television. She was wearing panties and nothing else. Not a sexy hot-date g-string, but the sort of plain, comfortable cotton panties that come in packs of three, all childish, ice-cream colors. The kind of panties a girl wears when she isn't planning for anyone to see them.

"Zandora?" I said, taking one of her manicured hands. I felt like I ought to take off the latex gloves, but I didn't. "Zandora, can you hear me?"

She looked up at me with no recognition in her pale

blue eyes. The left was nearly all pupil, a deep black hole rimmed in ice. That side of her head seemed to have gotten the worst of it. I don't know from head trauma, but even I could see that something was very, very wrong. Tears made thin clean tracks through the blood on her cheek and she whispered in slurred Romanian.

"Lenuta?" I said. "Lenuta, it's me, Angel."

"Angel?" she whispered. "I feel dizzy."

"Hang on, Lenuta," I told her. "We're gonna get you out of here, okay?"

"I can't…" she said.

Then she died. One second she was there and the next she just…wasn't. I felt cold and sick, unable to let go of her lukewarm hand.

"Lenuta," I said again, uselessly. "Lenuta."

I thought of the first time I'd met her, how sweet and raw she'd looked back then, before she'd gotten bleached, implanted, liposucked, French-manicured and Brazilian waxed into this generic, tan, platinum blonde lying here like a broken doll on the cheap beige carpet of a Vegas motel. I remembered helping her pick out the name Zandora Dior and giving her some backdoor hygiene tips for her big debut in *Fresh-N-Tight 7*. I remembered how nervous she was before her first scene with the freakishly endowed Monster Marcus Long and how she ended up dating him and eventually breaking his heart. I remembered coughing up her name when Jesse slugged me in the belly. I let go of her hand and got to my feet, feeling hollow and cold.

"Angel?" It was Malloy in the doorway. He was winded and bleeding from a split in his lip that mirrored mine almost exactly. "We need to get the hell out of here."

"Where's the other guy?" I asked.

"Fucker got away," Malloy said. "We better do the same."

"What about—"

I turned back to the redneck, whose face was turning purple. He wasn't finished dying yet. It seemed unfair, somehow, that he should outlive Zandora, even by a few minutes.

"*Now*, Angel," Malloy said.

I did what Malloy said, but not without one last glance back over my shoulder at the crumpled body that used to be a girl I knew.

10.

"Zandora's dead," Malloy said, the little Kia screeching out of the Silver Spur parking lot before I could even pull my door closed.

"Yeah," I said.

Malloy hung a sharp left that threw me against the passenger side door. I put on my seat belt with shaking hands.

"You okay?" he asked without looking at me.

I looked out the window at the tawdry, sun-bleached pawnshops and wedding chapels and tattoo parlors that we passed. "I'm fine."

Malloy made a soft wordless noise and I realized that I wasn't sure how to feel about him. I had never really been sure, but that cold, dead look I had seen in his eyes as he beat that thug stuck with me. Got under my skin. If I had seen hot rage or blood lust or something like that, I would have understood. After all, I knew what that felt like. If I could have beaten Jesse Black to death with my bare hands, I would have done it with a smile. But Malloy's strange, chilly blankness was profoundly disturbing. It reminded me that I didn't really know him. Malloy was all I had left of my old life, and I didn't really know him at all.

"Gloves," Malloy said, holding out one hand.

I peeled the latex gloves off my sweaty fingers and handed them over. Malloy crumpled them up and peeled off his own gloves, turning the last one inside out so my two and his left were neatly wrapped up inside the right. He pulled into a Burger King lot and parked far in the back, beside the dumpster and away from all the other cars.

"Want anything?" he asked, gesturing toward the restaurant.

I shook my head, queasy at the thought of eating after everything that had happened. My body still jangled with a kind of shaky, nauseous adrenaline hangover.

"Stay here," Malloy said, taking off his jacket, unbuckling his shoulder holster and depositing the tangled rig in my lap. The gun was heavy. "I don't want anybody to see you right now."

I nodded and held onto the gun. It didn't make me feel any safer.

I watched Malloy unbutton his blood-stained shirt and strip swiftly out of it, revealing thick, muscular arms and a white wife-beater undershirt that stretched taut over his hard, heavy gut. I had never met a man who actually wore an undershirt under a dress shirt. He had a Saint Michael medallion around his neck, a silver oval with a stamped image of a sword-wielding angel standing on a dragon. Malloy hadn't really struck me as the religious type, but then again, being half Irish and half Mexican, he kind of had the Catholic thing coming at him hard from both sides. Being Italian myself, I could sympathize, even though all that was left of my Catholic upbringing was a fondness for short plaid skirts. I wondered how he explained working with godless harlots like me and my girls to kindly father so-and-so at confession. Never mind that whole beating-a-guy-to-death-with-his-bare-hands business.

"I'm gonna go get cleaned up," Malloy said. "Give me your sweatshirt."

He got out of the car and tossed his shirt and jacket, my sweatshirt, and the balled-up gloves into the dumpster. He put the original rental plates back on the car, then crossed the lot and went into the Burger King.

While I waited, I watched a trio of fat women herding a batch of squabbling children out of a minivan and into the restaurant. It seemed strange and surreal to me, the way the rest of the world just kept on going in the background of this madness.

Malloy returned all pink and clean. He reached into the back seat and grabbed a loud Hawaiian shirt out of one of the bags from Target. The shirt featured a bright, busy pattern of rainbow-colored parrots and tropical drinks. He pulled off the price tag and slipped the shirt on.

"Here," he said, handing me another bag from Target. "I want you to change while I'm driving."

"Why?" I asked, looking into the bag. It contained a matronly beige jersey tank dress, a lightweight pink cardigan and flat pink shoes. To top it off, there was a horrible pink cloth sun hat.

"In case anyone saw us at the Silver Spur," he said, pulling a red baseball cap down snug over his silver buzz-cut. The hat said *FBI—Female Booty Inspector*. "How do I look?"

"Like a tourist," I said. It was almost impossible to believe this was the same man whose murderous, blank eyes had made me feel so cold.

"Perfect," he replied, getting back into the car and pulling out into the light midday traffic.

"Turn right here," I told him. "At this light."

"We have a pretty good window to hit Eye Candy before the Vegas PD," Malloy said, making the turn. "Zandora had the do-not-disturb sign up on the door so if nobody reports the racket we made, they might not find the bodies until she's supposed to check out."

I changed into the ugly clothes while Malloy drove, slipping the dress over my tank top and slithering out of my jeans beneath. I had plenty of practice changing in moving cars. Back when I was a teenager, I would routinely leave the house in some nice pastel good-girl disguise. Then as soon as I was out of Mama's sight, I would tease up my hair and wiggle into zebra-striped spandex, all in the back seat of a friend's car on the way to check out some cute guy's band at the Thirsty Whale.

While I got myself dressed up to match Malloy's tourist duds, we headed over to Eye Candy.

That place was in a class by itself, rivaling the biggest casinos for over-the-top excess. Like Disneyland with tits. It had opened after I was out of the game, so I'd never had the chance to dance there. My girls either loved it or hated it. The competition between the Eye Candy dancers was brutal and unrelenting, but for girls who were tough, ambitious and could take the heat, the money was ridiculous. Me, I probably wouldn't have lasted one song in a shark tank like that.

As we turned off the freeway, Eye Candy's huge, sprawling complex shimmered, mirage-like up ahead, a pink neon oasis of LIVE NUDE GIRLS in the midst of dusty industrial nothing. It was astounding, a self-contained multi-level biosphere of calculated titillation and shameless indulgence, open twenty-four hours a day, seven days a week. Once the marks were in, they basically never needed to leave. In addition to the massive main stage and six smaller go-go stages, there were also eight private VIP champagne lounges and six special fantasy rooms. There was a restaurant where you could be served overpriced steaks by beautiful girls in tiny cowgirl outfits. A sports bar where you could be served overpriced beer by beautiful girls in tiny bikinis. A cigar room where you could be sold overpriced cigars by beautiful girls in tiny g-strings. The only thing you couldn't do there was sleep. Or actually get laid.

Personally, I never understood the appeal of places like that. Eye Candy was a well-oiled machine that existed, like everything else in Vegas, for one reason only. To empty wallets. And once those wallets were empty there were three convenient cash machines to help fill them up again. Eye Candy didn't sell pussy. It sold the dream of pussy. It was an endless glittering tease, all fantasy with no real payoff. It seemed like a big waste of time and money better spent on an actual hooker, but hey, my girls cleaned up when they featured there so I couldn't really complain.

Malloy didn't want to valet park, so he drove right past the guy in the gold vest and around to the self-park area off to one side.

"Wait here," he said, just like he had said at the Burger King. I was getting tired of waiting, but I was also deeply grateful not to have to interact with anyone.

I watched Malloy walk over to the door of the club. As he went, I was amazed to see his usual wary body language loosen and open up. His hard, thuggish face went all soft and friendly, split wide by a big dopey grin. By the time he hit the door to the club, he had become every guy in every strip club in history.

A neckless lug in a tight tux patted Malloy down while he held his arms up in an affable sort of gee-whiz posture. He was then greeted by a leggy brunette in tiny peppermint-striped booty shorts and a pink Eye Candy baby doll t-shirt. She took his money and stamped his hand and as I watched her smile at Malloy and count out his change, I felt a swift spike of jealousy that took me completely by surprise. There was absolutely nothing between me and Malloy, but I still hated that girl in that moment. Not for her tan, aerobicized abs or her tight, muscular ass or any of a million other reasons women hate each other in this cutthroat *Cosmo* world we live in. I hated her for her pretty, perfect face. Her smooth lips and her straight nose and wide, bright eyes. My fingers went up to the swollen contours of my bruised and battered mug and I suddenly wanted to go rampaging through the club with a baseball bat, smashing every pretty face in the place.

I didn't. I waited.

Cars came and went. Men went in and out, both in groups and alone. Time passed and even though Malloy had chosen a shady parking spot, it still got real hot inside the car. I had all the windows down but there was no breeze at all. I peeled off the damp pink cardigan and fanned myself with a California roadmap.

About a hundred years later, Malloy came out. There was a fuchsia smear of lipstick on his unshaven cheek.

"Got it," he said, handing me a sheet of paper, tossing the baseball cap into the back seat and starting up the engine. "Know anyone who can read Romanian?"

I looked down at the paper. It was a faxed copy of Lia's handwritten note.

"How'd you get them to give this to you?"

"I didn't," Malloy replied as he pulled out of the lot. "I got lucky. While I was waiting in the office for the manager to show up and talk to me, I scrolled through the memory on the fax machine. Looks like they haven't erased it in ages. They probably don't even know how. Anyway, the fax from your office was still in there so I just reprinted it."

"What did you tell the manager when you saw him?" I asked. "When the cops find out that Zandora is dead, won't you be in trouble for asking about her?"

Malloy shook his head.

"Nah," he said, turning onto the freeway. "I just asked if Zandora was there. I said I wanted to talk to your models about you, that I was investigating your disappearance. The manager said Zandora wasn't in till the night shift and told me to come back later. I thanked him and left. Anybody see you?"

"I don't think so," I said.

"Hope you're right," Malloy replied. "I got a bad feeling this is gonna get pretty ugly."

11.

"Do you trust Didi?" Malloy asked me, pulling off the freeway and into the quiet streets of Burbank.

I had been asleep for most of the ride back from Vegas. Well, maybe asleep wasn't the right word. Dazed, out of it, shell-shocked and incapable of processing everything that had happened in the last twenty-four hours. I hadn't noticed the sun going down and felt disoriented to wake and find it fully dark outside. Malloy had gotten another cheap suit jacket out of the gym bag back in Vegas and at some point during the ride he must have taken it off and used it to cover me. It was warm and smelled like him, cigarettes and supermarket aftershave. I pulled it tighter around myself, bunching it up under my chin.

"Of course I trust Didi," I said. "I'd trust her with my life."

He nodded and took the turn into the car rental place across from the Burbank Airport. I huddled inside his big jacket as I waited outside the office. When he pulled around front in his own SUV, he got out, walked around to the passenger side and opened the door for me.

"Thanks," I said.

He punched some buttons on his cell phone, slipping on a hands-free rig as he pulled out of the rental place.

"Didi?" he said into the mike. "Malloy." He paused. "Yeah I know." He looked at me and then back at the road. "It's terrible. Listen, Didi, I'd like to talk to you about the case. Tonight. Get a pen."

He gave Didi his address just as we turned the corner onto his block.

"Twenty minutes," he said and ended the call.

Malloy's place was one of those little rundown fifties-era bungalow complexes in a so-so neighborhood, just off Hollywood Way. He drove past twice to make sure there was no surveillance before he pulled into the alley behind the complex and let me out, leaving the engine running.

"Go on," Malloy said, unlocking the door to his apartment and ushering me inside with one hand on the small of my back. "I'm gonna go park the car."

Inside his place it was immaculate and generic, like an IKEA showroom or a midrange hotel. No personal photos. No funny magnets on the fridge. No clutter of mail or books or DVDs. There was a sturdy gray couch and a black leather chair. A modest television in the corner and a blond wood coffee table with nothing on it. The kitchen was to the left through a doorless arch. It was narrow and yellow and very clean. At the far end, beneath the window, was a small aluminum table with a clean glass ashtray and a single chair. There were two closed doors, probably leading to the bedroom and bathroom.

It felt strange standing there alone in someone else's apartment. It made me miss my own little house.

Malloy returned a few minutes later.

"Make yourself at home," he said, setting his gun and shoulder rig on the coffee table. "But stay away from the windows."

"Okay," I said, but I didn't sit down. I just pulled Malloy's jacket tighter around myself.

There was a moment of awkward silence. I wondered suddenly who the last woman he'd brought to this apartment might have been.

"You want something?" Malloy asked, walking into the narrow kitchen and pulling open the fridge. "Water or a Diet Coke or something? I don't have any hard stuff."

"A Coke would be fine," I told him, thinking the caffeine might do me some good. Sharpen up the dull edges. "I don't drink the hard stuff anyway."

He looked back at me with a can of Diet Coke in one hand and a bottle of water in the other.

"You quit?" he asked.

"Never really started," I replied.

Malloy came back into the main room, handing me the can and twisting open the bottle of water for himself. He downed nearly half in one slug and wiped his mouth on the back of his hand, then touched the split in his lower lip with his thumb.

"I quit," he said.

Before I could think of anything to say about that, there was a rapid knock on the door. It was Didi. Malloy peered out through the blinds and gestured for me to step back through the archway and into the kitchen before he opened the door.

"Lalo," Didi said, throwing her arms around his neck and squeezing him tight. "God, can you believe this?" She let him go and then wrapped her arms around herself. "It's a fucking nightmare."

"Come on in," Malloy told her, pulling her into the

apartment and closing the door, engaging multiple locks.

Didi was wearing a shiny black mini-dress that was about ten years out of style and clung tight to her chubby curves. She had on sparkly silver high-heeled sandals and was clutching a little matching purse that she had packed to bursting. Her mouth was slicked a bright, candy apple red and her mascara was smudged beneath her eyes. She had obviously been on a date when Malloy had called. She and I were very much alike in that respect. When we were upset, we went out and got laid.

"Did you notice that you were followed?" Malloy asked, looking out through the blinds again. "A dark gray Caprice. Not very subtle."

"Those fucking cops," Didi said. "They're following me now?"

"Looks that way," Malloy said. "They're probably hoping Angel will try and contact you."

"Listen," Didi said. "About Angel—"

I couldn't stand to stay in the kitchen any longer.

"Didi," I said, stepping into the main room. "It's okay. I'm okay."

"Angel?" she said, rushing over to me. She looked me up and down, and her painted eyes went wide. "You call this okay? Holy shit, Angel, who did this to you?"

I couldn't speak, I just pulled the ugly hat off my head and twisted it in my hands. Didi threw her arms around me, stroking my hair. Every time her fingers would find some lump or scab she would curse under her breath, swearing she was going to kill whoever did this. Her perfume made me feel like sneezing and I felt uncomfortable being hugged, as if the fact that I had just watched two people die was all over my skin like the stink of that trash bag dress. And of course it hurt, too. But I didn't want her to let go.

"Lalo," Didi said. "You want to tell me what the hell is going on?"

Malloy gave Didi the Cliffs Notes version while Didi hung on to me like someone was going to try and take me away. When he was done, she sat down on the sofa and pulled me down next to her.

"Give me a cigarette," Didi said to Malloy.

Malloy took the pack out of his pocket and shook out the last two cigarettes. He parked one in his own mouth and handed the other to Didi.

"I thought you quit," I said as she accepted a light from Malloy.

"Fuck that," she said, sucking smoke like it was oxygen. She ran her fingers through her hair and exhaled slowly. "What are we going to do?"

"First off," Malloy said. "We need a cover story so I can talk to people without raising too much suspicion. I want you to tell everyone you hired me as a private investigator to find out what happened to Angel. I'll need you to write me a check for my services. I'll cash it and then give you the money back but I want a solid paper trail between us. That'll explain this visit for your buddies in the Caprice." He lit his own cigarette. "Also, people will be more likely to talk to me if they think I'm asking on your behalf."

"If you find the fuckers who did this, you can keep the money," she said. "What about Angel?"

"What about me?" I asked.

"She needs to keep a low profile," Malloy said. "As

soon as the guy that got away in Vegas reports back to his boss, then the boss is gonna know Angel isn't dead. He'll be looking for her too."

"Jesus," Didi said softly. "Jesus, this is bad."

The three of us were silent for a stretch, all contemplating how bad it really was.

"Didi," Malloy said, breaking the silence finally, "can you tell me everything you remember about the blonde with the briefcase?"

"You know, it's funny," Didi said. "After I left the office, I started thinking about her. I was pretty sure I recognized her. I'm sure she's done videos, but I can't remember the name she went by or the name of the series I saw her in. It was some super-low-budget amateur line. Mostly girl/girl and solo toy stuff but I'm pretty sure the one I saw her in was a boy/girl scene. It think it had 'teen' in the title."

"Great," I said, "That narrows it down to about seven billion."

"It was a real boring title," Didi said. "Very generic."

"*Teen Pleasures*?" I suggested. "*Teen Tryouts*? *Teen Cream*? *Teen Beaver*?"

"No." She shook her head. "It was more like *Horny Teens* or *Dirty Teens*." She turned to Malloy. "You got Internet access in this joint?"

He nodded and gestured with his chin toward one of the two closed doors.

"In there," he said. "But I don't know if I want to go surfing a bunch of teen smut on my PC. Won't I get logged by the FBI or something?"

" 'Teen' just means girls with no implants and an amateur look," I said. "There's nothing illegal about adult videos featuring girls that are over eighteen and besides, most of those girls are older than they look. I was twenty-one when I did *Teen Temptations*."

Malloy shrugged.

"I don't know," he said. "Me, I like real women. You know, grownups."

Didi flashed him a smile and stood, smoothing her tight skirt.

"Well," she said. "We'll discuss that later, honey." She winked and took my hand. "Come on."

Inside Malloy's predictably spartan bedroom was a small metal and glass desk with an inexpensive laptop sitting beside a jar of pens, a small printer and a cordless telephone. There was just the one chair so Didi and I sat on the bed behind Malloy like backseat drivers.

A Google search for the word "Teen" plus "Adult" and "DVD" gave us a staggering 20,000,000 hits.

"Forget that shit," Didi said. "Try slutfinder.com."

Malloy shook his head as he typed.

"Right," Didi said. "Pick the 'amateur' category and then put 'teen' in the title field."

"Jesus," he said as his screen filled with flashing photos of teen beaver. I could see the muscles in his jaw bunch up as he watched the screen.

"What?" I asked.

"This," he said, gesturing with his chin. "I don't know about this shit."

"What's not to know?" I said. "It's just pussy. It won't bite you."

Malloy didn't respond and I felt myself starting to get hot and defensive. The last thing I needed just then was some moralistic argument about the evils of smut.

"You're not getting squeamish on us, are you Lalo?" Didi asked.

"It's just..." He shrugged.

"You got something to say," I told him. "Say it."

"Well, look at this girl here." He pointed to a skinny blonde on the cover of a DVD titled *Goodbye Seventeen*. "She's still got braces on her teeth, for chrissake."

"A lot of the amateur girls get braces," I said. "It's a better investment than implants and the guys love it."

"That's sick," Malloy muttered, clicking away swarming pop-ups with lurid headlines like TEEN TWATS WANT YOUR SPUNK NOW!!! and SEE WHITE TRASH TEEN TRAMPS TAKE ON THE TEAM! "I mean, don't get me wrong, I'm all for dirty movies, but this...I don't know. I know it's legal, but I just don't think it's right for a man my age to be looking at girls that seem so young. Christ, half these girls look younger than my daughter."

"I never knew you had a daughter," Didi said.

"Yeah," Malloy said. "Her name's Paloma. She was eighteen back in April."

He took a drag off his cigarette and looked away from the images on the screen. He opened a desk drawer and pulled out a posed school photo and handed it to Didi. I peered over Didi's shoulder. The girl in the photo was plain and a little heavy and looked way too much like Malloy to be considered particularly attractive, but she had a crooked smart-ass grin that I liked. She looked like she wouldn't take any shit from anyone. I wondered why Malloy had never mentioned her.

"She looks like a real smart kid," Didi said, handing the photo back to Malloy.

"She lives with her mom out in Santa Fe," Malloy said,

looking at the photo for a second and then putting it back in the drawer, face down. "We're not all that close." He looked back up at the screen. "But I sure as hell wouldn't want a bunch of dirty old men jacking off over her on the Internet." He closed the drawer. "You think these girls don't have fathers too?"

I frowned and stood up.

"Yeah, well, these girls are all legal, consenting adults," I said, taking Malloy's jacket off and tossing it on the bed beside me. "Whether their daddies like it or not."

"You can't tell me something called *Teenage Nympho Cheerleaders* isn't meant to get older guys off on the idea of nailing underage high school girls," Malloy said. "It's like one step away from statutory rape."

"It's a hell of a step," I said. I was really angry now. "It's just a fantasy. What are you, the thought police?"

"Come on, now," Malloy started to say but I cut him off.

"Besides, who the hell are you to be getting all high and mighty about what's right and wrong after…"

I had to stop myself before I said another word or things were really going to get out of hand. I turned away and tried to get a handle on my anger. I wished that I could stop being so defensive about all this. Malloy was probably right that some of the teen videos went a little too far. It's not like he was criticizing me personally. But I was feeling fragile and ugly and couldn't seem to help taking Malloy's distaste as a personal attack. Plus, my own father broke my jaw when he found out about my videos, so my sympathy for fathers who don't approve of their daughters doing porn is basically nonexistent.

"Listen…" he started to say, but Didi could see it was getting ugly and quickly cut him off.

"Enough, already," she said. "Knock it off, Mr. Fucking Sensitive and just read off the damn titles. You want to find that blonde or don't you?"

Malloy was silent for a handful of seconds and so was I. I looked down at the back of Malloy's flushed neck and I realized abruptly that this little spat was the most Malloy had revealed about himself since I'd known him. I think he knew it too and was regretting it.

"Right," he said and started reading off the list of titles on the screen.

Listening to Malloy read off titles like *Teen Cum Dumpsters* or *Pop My Tight Teen Poop Chute* in his gravelly, deadpan voice was suddenly way funnier than it had any right to be. I had been sulky and pissed off just seconds before and now I was fighting to repress a fit of crazy giggles. I was afraid to start laughing. I might never stop.

"There," Didi said, getting to her feet and putting a hand on Malloy's shoulder. "Click on *Dirty Teens*."

Turned out there were only three DVDs in the *Dirty Teens* series. Didi was pretty sure the DVD she'd seen the blonde in had a high number.

"Try *Naughty Teens*," Didi said.

There were twenty-one DVDs in that series and the box covers were cheap and inept, all bad Photoshop and tacky yellow titles. I didn't recognize any of the girls but they were all very similar. Wan, pale and sickly. Probably junkies. All natural and all very young looking. Each one had a bland, unimaginative GND name like Beth or Tracy or Heather. No last names.

"There she is," Didi cried triumphantly when Malloy clicked on number seventeen.

She was right. The blonde who had called herself "Lia" and wriggled out my bathroom window was prominently featured on the cover of *Naughty Teens 17*. She was billed as "Kimberly" and she had a male friend posing with her in the photo. A very close friend, apparently. The friend's head was blocked by the 'g' in *Naughty* but I didn't need to see his head to recognize him instantly. I felt a sick flush of anger.

"Jesse Black," Didi said. "Motherfucker."

12.

"Okay, ladies," Malloy said. "We need a plan of action."

"We need to find Jesse fucking Black and cut his goddamn nuts off," Didi said. "How's that for a plan of action?"

"As satisfying as that might be," Malloy said. "I advise we start by figuring out what the hell is really going on here. We'll get to Jesse eventually, but I don't want anybody going off half cocked."

There was some kind of a dirty joke in there somewhere, but I was too exhausted to make the reach.

"What about the note?" I said instead. "We need to get someone who can translate Lia's note."

"Someone who can keep quiet about it," Malloy added.

"Wanda Curtis?" Didi suggested.

"I think she's Hungarian, not Romanian" I said. "What about Honey Westlake?"

Didi snorted.

"The only time Honey Westlake is quiet is when she has a dick in her mouth," she said. "Might as well put it on the six o'clock news."

"Tabitha Moore," I said. "She's Romanian, right?"

"Right," Didi agreed. "Tabby's a decent kid."

"There's really that many Romanian chicks in porn?" Malloy asked.

"Romanian, Czech, Hungarian," Didi replied, "It's like these Eastern European girls are taking over the industry. They look like supermodels and they'll do double anal with no condom for five bucks. Makes it nearly impossible to get decent treatment for American girls."

"No shit," Malloy said.

"Come on," I said. "Not all Eastern European girls are like that. I mean, look at Zandora..."

I bit my lower lip. Nobody said anything. The screen of Malloy's computer kept flashing lurid, fleshy images.

"What do you know about the guys who put out *Naughty Teens*?" Malloy asked, gently changing the subject. He squinted and read off the screen "PDM Productions."

"PDM's one of those companies that buys amateur content from independent producers," Didi said. "You know, guys in Idaho shooting their girlfriend and her gal pals making out after too many diet beers. PDM buys the raw footage, edits it down, and sells it as *Heartland Hos 23*."

"So how can we find out who made *Naughty Teens*?" Malloy asked. "And who this Kimberly chick really is?"

Didi and I both looked at each other and spoke simultaneously.

"Two-two-five-seven."

Malloy frowned.

"US Code Title 18 section 2257," Didi said, wrinkling her nose. "The so-called 'child protection' act."

"That's something to do with record keeping, right?" Malloy asked.

"It's basically just another way to make life hard for godless smut peddlers," I said. "Now not only do you have to have all your drivers licenses for all your talent—scanned, not just photocopied—but you also have to put your physical address on the beginning of every DVD and on every Web site. Not a PO box, but the actual physical location where the records are kept. You also need to put a real legal name as the custodian of records and guarantee that person will be at the listed address to make the records available for a minimum of four hours every business day. There's more, but that's the part that's gonna help us."

"God," Didi said. "I never thought I'd see the day when I'd be grateful for 2257."

"Right," Malloy said. "So if we go out and rent *Naughty Teens 17*, we'll get the address of the guy who made the video?"

"No," I said. "We'll probably just get the address of the PDM office. But what we can do is show up during the allotted four hours and get a drivers license for Kimberly or Lia or whatever her name is."

"Outstanding," Malloy said.

"What else?" Didi asked.

Malloy reached into the desk drawer and took out another pack of cigarettes. He offered one to Didi and she took it, letting him light it for her and then fanning the smoke away from me with one ring-heavy hand.

"Well," Malloy said. "I don't know about you, but I'd like to know what happened to that briefcase."

"Who cares," I asked. "For all we know, they've found it already."

"If they had," Malloy said. "They wouldn't have gone after Zandora. You want to know what I think?" He lit a cigarette for himself. "I think the blonde hid the briefcase somewhere in your office, probably in the bathroom, and then someone else found it, after the first round of goons had split but before they went back to toss your place while you were at the phony shoot." He sucked smoke and squinted at Didi. "You don't have it, do you, Didi?"

"Fuck off, Lalo," Didi said. "If I had it, don't you think I would have mentioned it by now?"

Malloy shrugged.

"Just asking," he said.

"So who all was in the office that day?" I asked. "It was pretty busy wasn't it?"

"Yeah," Didi said. "I'm so frazzled right now, though, I can barely remember."

"Got a surveillance system in your office?" Malloy asked.

I shook my head.

"I'm pretty sure there's a security camera in the lobby," Didi said. "I have no idea who keeps the tapes."

"I'll see what I can find out," Malloy said.

No one said anything for several minutes. Malloy and Didi smoked. I looked at the image of Jesse Black on the screen. My head hurt.

"Okay, look," Malloy said, crushing out his cigarette. "I think we oughta call it a night. Didi, remember what I said. Spread the word that you're paying me to look for Angel."

"Sure," Didi said, taking my hand. "I just hate to leave you alone, honey, what with everything that's happened."

"I'm not alone," I said. "I got Malloy."

"Okay," Didi said, "But the next time I come by, I'll bring some ginger snaps or something."

"I don't think it's a good idea for you to come by again," Malloy said, shaking his head. "It's too risky."

"Are you sure?" Didi asked. "I mean…"

"I'll stay in contact by phone," Malloy replied, gently taking Didi's arm and maneuvering her toward the door.

"I'll be fine, Didi," I said, wondering if that were really true.

"Okay then, honey," Didi said. She reached out and grabbed Malloy's wrist. "You watch over her good, you big lug, or you'll have me to answer to."

"You got it," Malloy said.

I stayed in Malloy's bedroom while he let Didi out. After a few minutes of doing things I couldn't see, Malloy came back into the bedroom with a Thai takeout menu. It felt weird to be alone with him again and I felt strangely self-conscious about sitting on his bed. The cover image for *Naughty Teens 17* was still on the screen of his laptop.

"You want me to order some food for you?" he asked.

I looked up at him standing there holding the menu and I was hit with a sudden powerful urge to pull him down on the bed with me. It was a bad idea and I knew it, but I always react to stress that way. I looked down at my hands.

"What about you?" I asked. "You're not hungry?"

"I don't want to order enough food for two people now that Didi's gone," Malloy said "It would look suspicious." I've got stuff to eat in the fridge. You know, guy food. Lunch meat. Frozen stuff. Nothing I'd offer to a guest."

"It's okay," I said. "I'm not hungry."

"You oughta have something," Malloy said.

I wanted him to put down the menu and put those big, calloused hands up my skirt. I wanted him to get rough, to make me forget.

But I was still pretty sore from my date with Jesse. It

was good to have that as an excuse not to make a pass because I really didn't want to think about the fact that I wasn't all that sexy anymore. The fact that Malloy would probably be totally turned off if I came on to him. At best he'd feel sorry for me.

"No thanks," I said instead. "I'm fine."

Malloy nodded.

"Well," he said. "If you change your mind later you can go ahead and help yourself."

I wondered if he was still talking about food.

13.

Although I was exhausted, I was way too jittery to really sleep. I dozed on and off on Malloy's couch all night, flickering television inanity unable to compete with the jumbled emotions in my head. It didn't help that I seemed to be on virtually every channel, more so on the flashy, shallow "entertainment" news shows than the supposedly legit outlets, but even the almighty CNN seemed to be unable to resist running a few carefully cropped clips from *Double Dare* and footage of me at the AVN awards with a very young Jenna Jameson. They also showed a ton of footage of the two cops who seemed to be in charge of bringing me to justice. One was black and a little nerdy-looking and tended to keep his mouth shut. The other was white, blond and athletic and looked like an actor playing a cop. The camera loved him.

But the footage that really got under my skin was a quick shot of Sam's wife Georgie looking pale and numb as she was hustled from a car to some dull, official-looking building. Sweet, busty, hippy-dippy Georgie who wouldn't hurt a fly and really honestly believed that love could change the world. I guess she had learned the hard way that the opposite number was much more efficient. Not hate of course, which is sort of like love's twisted sibling, but cold, heartless disregard for human life.

Sam had told me that the man who set up the phony shoot "had Georgie" but he clearly didn't have her anymore. Had he just let her go after he had her husband killed? I suddenly wanted desperately to find Georgie and talk to her, find out what she knew, what had really happened, but the fact that she probably believed I had killed Sam left a hollow ache under my ribs.

I searched around the channels for an old movie with no commercials. Something sweet and silly with no guns. I found a musical with Cyd Charisse and turned the sound down low, trying not to think. It didn't work.

I couldn't get a fix on how to feel about Malloy. I wanted to slug him and fuck him and get away from him and be rescued by him all at the same time. I felt surrounded by him, here in his place where everything smelled like he did. I wondered why he was going out of his way like this to help me—he didn't know me that well and certainly didn't owe me anything. I wondered if he was sleeping on the other side of the bedroom door, or lying awake like me. I couldn't decide if I wanted to creep into his bedroom or sneak out the door, so I just stayed on the couch and pulled my knees up to my chin.

I didn't know if I wanted Malloy or not, but I did know the one thing I really wanted. Sure, I wanted revenge and I wanted to clear my name, but more than anything else, I just wanted to go home.

If I had lost everything in a flood or an earthquake, I would be sad, but I could eventually let it all go and find a way to start over. But my things weren't destroyed. They were sitting there in my house, just the way I left them. The coffee cup I hadn't washed. Fruit from the farmer's market that would just go bad. The book I was reading. My dirty laundry. My vibrator—God, did I leave it on the bed or put it back in the drawer? Would the cops staking out the place bother to water my plants?

Worse, what was going to happen to my little house on Morrison Street now that I was a fugitive, wanted for murder? I'd never had a relationship that lasted even a tenth as long as my relationship with my house, my own private sanctuary where everything was just the way I liked it. When I bought that house, it was a cheap 70s fixer-upper with ugly shag carpet and a leaky chimney. I gutted the place and redid everything from the ground up, made it my own. My mortgage was less than three years from being fully paid off. And didn't the cops seize your property if you were involved in a criminal investigation? I wasn't sure, but it killed me to think that after all the money and hard work I'd put into that place, those bastards could take it away just like that. Somehow, that hurt much more than what Jesse had done to me.

When the sun finally came up, Malloy came out of the bedroom. He was wearing gray sweatpants and a clean white t-shirt and he didn't look tired or rumpled or like he had just woken up. He looked the same as ever. I must have looked awful with my hair all snarled and sticky black eyes squinting against the sun. I felt like deep-fried shit.

"Coffee?" he asked, unfazed as he ambled into the kitchen. "Sorry, I don't have any Sweet'N Low."

"Black is fine," I said. "Do you mind if I jump in the shower?"

"Go right ahead," Malloy said, his wide back to me as he filled the carafe of the coffeemaker with bottled water. "You'll find clean towels in the cabinet to the left of the sink."

Malloy's bathroom was pristine and nearly empty. I carefully avoided looking into the mirror and concentrated on snooping around instead. You can tell a lot about a bachelor by his bathroom. Apparently Malloy was completely immune to the latest craze for marketing XXXTREME ultra-studly chick-magnet grooming products to insecure men. The last bachelor bathroom that I had been in had been cluttered with body spray and shower gel and crotch deodorant with names like JACKHAMMER, MAGMA FORCE, or BLAST OFF. Not here. Beside the faucet on the tiny sink was a bottle of store-brand antibacterial hand soap. Nothing else. Malloy's medicine cabinet contained no surprises. There was nothing odd, unique or amusing anywhere to be found. No Viagra or Rogaine or Preparation H. No Vicodin or Prozac or AZT. He could have been anybody.

Inside the shower stall, the white tile looked as sterile as an operating theater. The stainless steel gleamed. On a narrow, built-in shelf sat a bottle of dandruff shampoo and a plain white soap dish containing a large green-and-white bar of Irish fucking Spring. I didn't realize they still made that shit.

I stripped down and turned on the hot water in the shower. While I waited for it to warm up, I lost the battle to avoid looking in the mirror.

I guess you could say it was getting better, but it was still horrible. The swelling had gone down and my right eye, which had been swollen almost completely shut, was now open. The color palette of my bruises had shifted from lurid purple to more muted tones of ochre and bile. I wasn't going to be winning any beauty contests any time soon.

The water was hot by then so I slipped in and goddamn, that was good. It was the first real shower I'd had since Jesse and it did wonders to improve my mood. By the time I was done, I almost felt like I could beat the bastards who did this to me. I felt like I could win. Must have been the Irish Spring.

When I got out I found a black mug of black coffee waiting for me on the coffee table. Malloy was sitting at the kitchen table, reading the paper.

"Hey," I said softly, pulling the white towel tighter around my body and picking up the mug. "What should I wear? The dress or the jeans?"

I don't know why I asked. I was a big girl and I'd been dressing myself without Malloy's advice for more than 35 years. In spite of everything, it was still way too easy to cast Malloy in the hero/Daddy role. I really needed to watch that.

He looked up at me and the fact that I was only wearing a towel registered in his eyes. He looked back down at the paper. I scanned his face for any reaction at all, any tiny hint of a response to my near nakedness. He hid it well, but there was an undeniable tension in his jaw and shoulders. It could have been any number of things, but I desperately wanted it to be desire. It was as if I needed some kind of proof that I was still just a little bit sexy in spite of everything. Realizing that I had been fishing for a reaction, I felt suddenly pathetic, like a junkie combing the carpet for a dropped crumb of dope.

"For now just put the jeans and tank top from yesterday morning back on," he said, sipping his coffee without looking up, giving away nothing. "I have an idea."

That's how I wound up dressed like a boy.

14.

Malloy pulled the SUV into the lot of a shabby North Hollywood mini-mall that contained a purified water retailer, a 98-cent store, a restaurant that offered "*especialidades Oaxaqueños*," and a tiny barbershop. Malloy took a spot in front of the barber.

There was a Spanish sign above the door. The window featured a sinister, weirdly proportioned painting depicting a pair of floating scissors hovering behind the small, disembodied head of what looked like a child with a mustache.

"Are you sure about this?" I asked, running my fingers nervously through my hair. Malloy had made me cut off my long nails at his apartment and my newly blunt fingers felt foreign against my scalp. "You know, I'm about as far from a boy as you can get without being pregnant."

"Sure I'm sure," Malloy said, taking my arm. "Come on."

"It's closed," I said, pointing to a hand-lettered sign that read *CERRADO*. "It's a Sunday, isn't everyone supposed to be at church?"

"I called ahead," Malloy said. "He's expecting us."

Inside, the shop smelled like the air had been sealed in a jar since 1947. Cigarettes and pomade and Clubman shaving talc and that blue stuff the combs sit in to kill germs. The barber himself was an ancient brown gnome with a face like a dried apple and a shiny bald head. He wore an immaculate white short-sleeved *guayabera* and white shorts that showed off bandy little rooster legs with large knobby knees. I wondered briefly about the wisdom of trusting a bald barber, but Malloy seemed to think the guy was all right.

"Jarocho's been cutting my hair for twenty years," Malloy said, patting the barber's stooped shoulder. "He's solid."

The barber grinned, flashing a set of dazzlingly fake white choppers and said something to Malloy in rapid-fire Spanish. Malloy replied and the two of them went back and forth for a few minutes. I had no idea what they were talking about. I studied a large faded travel poster for Veracruz, feeling awkward and uncomfortable. I noticed another even older guy snoring softly in a cheap kitchen chair in the far corner of the shop. He looked like a mummy, but he had a full, luxurious head of snow-white hair done up in a mile-high 50's era pompadour that probably hadn't changed since it was invented.

The barber leaned over and fingered my hair, shaking his head. I figured he was telling Malloy it was a shame to cut such pretty hair. Didn't I know it.

"I told him you were hiding out from an abusive boyfriend," Malloy told me. "He'll take good care of you."

I nodded, still unable to calm a chilly electric anxiety that wouldn't leave me alone.

"I'm gonna hit the thrift store across the street and get you some clothes," Malloy said, not waiting for an answer before he turned to leave.

I shook my head. After the initial surprise of the nice jeans, I was starting to get a little tired of having Malloy as my personal shopper.

The barber sat me down in one of two ancient red vinyl

barber chairs, whipping a blue plastic cape around my shoulders with dramatic flair.

"You no worry," he told me with a wink.

"Right," I said.

Jarocho made with the scissors and when my thick dark tresses started falling to the scuffed green linoleum I had a moment of irrational panic. I wanted to call the whole thing off. Wasn't I already ugly enough? But it was too late. The barber thumbed on a bulky old electric clipper that looked like something they'd use to shave dogs before neutering and started running it up the back of my head. Before I knew it I had a buzz cut identical to Malloy's. All of the dyed chocolate-cherry curls were gone, leaving behind only a quarter inch of natural salt and pepper roots. I was horrified by how much gray I had.

Malloy returned then with two cheap plastic shopping bags. I was almost afraid to look inside.

I guess I had been hoping for some kind of classy, androgynous Marlene Dietrich sort of suit or something, but Malloy had other ideas.

The first bag contained several extra large t-shirts, including a Lakers shirt, and a pair of baggy men's jeans. I hadn't told Malloy that Lia had been wearing a Lakers shirt the last time I saw her and although this one was a different style, it made me feel a little weird. I decided I would wear one of the other ones.

"The big mistake people make when they do drag is going too far." Malloy said. "Overcompensating. Too girly. Too macho. If you want to be believable, you have to keep it simple. Nothing for the eye to catch on."

I wondered if Malloy had ever done drag. I tried to

imagine some elaborate Ed Wood-style sting operation that would require him to go undercover in angora, but somehow I just couldn't picture it. He handed me the other bag. It contained two large Ace bandages.

"Use one of those bandages to bind your chest," Malloy told me. "And wrap the other loosely around your waist."

"Around my waist?" I asked. "What for?"

"You've got a very small waist," he told me. "You need to bulk it up and make it closer to the size of your hips and chest. Make your shape less feminine." He looked down at my feet. "Your sneakers are fine."

I ducked into the closet-sized john, skinned out of my tank top and bra, and went to work battening down the twins. It was uncomfortable and I started sweating right away. I wrapped the other bandage around my waist until I wound up with a sort of dumpy sausage shape from the armpits to the hips.

Was it possible to make me feel less attractive? I knew being attractive was a liability on the lam but I missed it like a dry drunk misses that warm, happy Saturday night buzz. I was so used to the appreciative glances of men that I felt lost without that constant validation. I hardly knew who I was anymore.

When I was dressed, I came out of the tiny bathroom and glanced in the wall of mirrors at the boy I had become.

It almost worked. The hair was perfect, the silhouette unobtrusive beneath the loose clothing. The double shiner helped, too, and so did the broken nose. The big problem was my eyebrows.

I normally go through a good amount of monthly suffering in the ongoing war against my hairy Mediterranean genes. In addition to lip waxing (to keep me from sporting a mustache like Nonna Vincenza) and bikini waxing (I get the Playboy, not the Brazilian, since I know you're wondering), I also regularly wax my heavy eyebrows into slender, delicate arches. Very femme and very not-a-boy.

"I could try filling my eyebrows in thicker with an eye pencil," I said.

Malloy looked at my reflection in the mirror and shrugged.

"I'll just tell people you're gay," he said. "That you're my nephew who just moved out to L.A. and got bashed by a bunch of douchebags right in front of his apartment. I'll tell 'em I promised my sister I'd let you stay with me until they catch the guys who did it. That you're scared to be alone so I let you tag along."

Jarocho said something in Spanish to Malloy that got them both laughing.

"What?" I asked, feeling irritable and annoyed and left out.

"He says he would go gay for you," Malloy said.

I rolled my eyes.

"Great," I said.

Jarocho flashed his dentures and gave me two thumbs up.

The next order of business was to translate the note. Malloy gave me a wad of cash and then checked in with Didi by phone while I ducked into a nearby beauty supply store for some cheap non-prescription color contacts to disguise my black coffee eyes.

On impulse, I also bought a bleaching kit for my hair. Just because I was a boy didn't mean I had to put up with gray hair. I figured bleached blond would be about as far from my normal look as I could get and would be still reasonably believable for a gay guy my age.

Born actress that I was, I started imagining details about my new character. I figured I used to be a hot little twink ten years ago, but now I was getting older and thicker in the middle. My boyfriend of five years had just dumped me so I was overcompensating with the blond hair. I did a drag show on the weekends using the name Ivana Mandalay, which would explain the girly eyebrows. Of course, coming up with a believable real name was a little harder. I didn't want anything too butch, too silly, or over the top. I needed something generic and easy to remember.

"Daniel," I told Malloy when I got back in the car. "That's my new name."

Daniel was the name of the first guy who ever put his finger inside me. Danny Zawadski. He was big and blond, and stuttered when he was nervous. I think he's married now and owns a restaurant in the old neighborhood. Not a drag queen by any stretch of the imagination.

"Daniel?" Malloy said, looking me up and down. "That works." He looked down at the bag in my lap. "What else did you buy?"

"Bleach," I said. "I figured I should have blond hair to go with my new blue eyes."

"Right," Malloy said.

I wondered if he was pissed at me for improvising.

I don't know why, but I got a peculiar thrill from being off Malloy's script. I was really counting on him way too much. It felt good to make decisions for myself.

"Didi said that Romanian broad is on a shoot today," Malloy said. "But that we can meet her on the set at three when they break for lunch. In the meantime, we can go back to my place. You can do your hair and get those contacts in."

I wondered how many more different people I would need to be before I could be me again.

15.

Tabitha Moore's shoot was for Rawkus. They were set up in their dusty, cavernous studio on Stagg Ave. I never shot for Rawkus, since they don't pay for shit and I don't care for their creepy, misogynistic and insulting titles. *Filthy Fuckpigs. Whores Can't Say No.* Or their most popular series, *She Needs the Money.* I was actually a little surprised that Tabby was shooting for them, but she had always been one of the most cheerfully rowdy girls I'd ever met. She loved doing things just for the shock value and was famous for enthusiastic dirty talk that would make Max Hardcore blush. With her triple D implants and her voracious sexual stamina, Tabby was the Gonzo Queen of Over-The-Top town and didn't care who knew it.

Unsurprisingly, they were shooting a gang bang scene. The set was a half-assed mock-up of a locker room and a few of the guys had on random, contradictory pieces of athletic gear and various mismatched team uniforms. The parts of Tabby I could see between the seething tangle of male bodies seemed to be half dressed in a torn cheerleader outfit. I remembered Malloy's comment the night before about *Teenage Nympho Cheerleaders* and statutory rape. Cheerleader costume notwithstanding, nobody was ever going to mistake Tabby for a teenager. She had been in the business for seven years. Years in porn are like a lot like dog years. They tend to age the girls much quicker than normal human years. Tabby was only twenty-four but she already had more surgical enhancement than a Beverly Hills divorcee twice her age. She was a legendary party girl too, with a pill habit the size of Nevada, and whenever she started to run low on painkillers she'd just pop in for another procedure. Still, underneath it all, she was a good kid. I don't know if I would call her completely trustworthy, but she was all we had.

There were maybe five guys actively working the various stations of Tabby's anatomy while another six or seven stood back on standby, keeping their pumps primed and waiting to be rotated in. One funny thing about working in porn is how quickly you get used to seeing guys jack off. When I first started out, I couldn't stop staring. It gave me a nasty kind of thrill I can't quite explain, seeing something that was supposed to be this shameful secret done in such a public, nonchalant sort of way. I was fascinated by the wide variety of techniques and the odd, individual quirks each guy seemed to have to get the job done. But that didn't last. By my fifth or sixth film, I barely even noticed it anymore, unless the shoot was on standby, waiting for wood. Veteran cops and paramedics are unfazed by the sight of sucking chest wounds or decomposed babies. Porn pros don't bat an eye at the sight of six guys standing around yanking their cranks.

Malloy only had two months in country and was clearly not quite used to it yet. As we stood on the sidelines, waiting for them to finish up and call lunch, I could see in his body language that all this wanking made him itchingly uncomfortable. A lot of guys imagine that it would be this big turn-on to visit a porn set. My advice is, unless you really love watching other men jack off, don't bother.

Malloy turned away from the action and from me and walked quietly over to stand near the director. The director was young and morose with a large shaved head and a scruffy, chinless face like a strung-out fetus. He didn't seem to be paying any attention to the action. He sat alone and hunched over by the monitor, picking at a large scab on the back of his hand.

The cameraman was the one running the show. He was older, fat and beery with a backwards baseball hat and an oily little ponytail. Sweating profusely as he hovered around the fleshy jumble like a woozy fly, he droned on and on in a wet, nasal voice about how great everything was.

"Tito," the cameraman said. "Grab her hair. Great. Keep going. Now Tabby, can you raise your left leg up a little higher? Great. Keep going. Nick, trade places with Drew. Great. Keep going."

I felt sorry for the editor who was going to have to replace all that audio. I also felt sorry for Tabby, who was giving it 110 percent and would probably wind up with dreary stock music over all her saucy, creative dialog because that asshole camera guy wouldn't shut up.

A very deep man's voice spoke softly to my left, startling me.

"Hey."

I turned and saw that it was Dick Dallas. He had debuted just as I was getting out and we had never worked together, but we knew a lot of the same people. He was bigger than ever, shredded muscle on top of muscle and his formerly handsome face was becoming distorted and caveman-craggy from excessive use of steroids and Human Growth Hormone. He had a deep, leathery tan the color of barbeque sauce and had dyed his hair a dull, monochrome black. It kind of looked like he had gotten those hair implants, but I didn't want to look closely enough to be sure. He was wearing nothing but sneakers and was very happy to see me. I didn't take it personally. I knew it was just the Caverject. My breath caught as I waited for him to recognize me. Amazingly, he didn't.

"Are you okay?" he asked instead.

That was not at all what I had been expecting. The genuine concern in his face and voice seemed almost funny coming from a big hunky guy standing there naked with a hard-on.

"I'm fine," I replied, trying to pitch my voice as low as possible.

"Did he do this to you?" Dick asked, frowning as he gestured with his chin toward Malloy.

"Oh," I said. "Uh…no." I dug around in my brain for my cover story. "Some guys beat me up in front of my apartment, so I'm staying with my uncle until they get caught. He used to be a cop, my uncle. I was, y'know, scared to be alone so…"

"Son of a bitch," Dick said, shaking his blocky head. "Those spineless fucks don't dare try shit like that with me. Instead they gang up on a little guy like you to prove they're real men. Bastards." He put a hand on my shoulder, leaving a greasy lube spot on my t-shirt. "What's your name?"

"Daniel," I said, looking at my feet and flinching away from the large, bobbing erection threatening to poke me in the kidney. Dick Dallas never was the sharpest tool in the shed, but I still couldn't believe he didn't recognize me.

"Well, I'll tell you what, Daniel," he replied. "If you ever feel like you need someone to talk to, a shoulder to cry on..."

"Dick!" the cameraman called. "We're ready for you."

"Right," Dick called back over his shoulder. He turned to me with a wry, *it's a living* sort of shrug and then made his finger and thumb into the shape of a gun and pointed at me. "Catch you later."

The second his massive back was turned I burst out into silent stifled giggles behind my hand. My first day as a gay man and I'd already been cruised. Of course, Dick Dallas would pretty much fuck anything that didn't pull a knife on him. Still, I had to admit that it felt good to be desired, to be thought of as attractive again. The last person who'd thought I was sexy was Jesse.

The shoot continued through a few more rotations. I was feeling itchy and uncomfortable under my binder and the disturbingly familiar smell of sex and sweat and fruity body spray and cheap lube all baking under hot lights in an old dusty warehouse was a powerful reminder of why I got out from in front of the camera in the first place.

"Okay kids," the cameraman said. "Snap crackle pop. Who's ready?"

Of course it was Dick Dallas who led the pack.

"Come on all of you hot fuckers!" Tabby cried in her unique, un-American syntax that never failed to make me smile. "I must taste all of the cums right now in my face!"

One by one, each guy came forward and earned his

check. There were a few stragglers who held things up, taking longer than the rest to get to the point, but eventually the last guy did the job and the cameraman zoomed into Tabby's wide open mouth.

"...and cut," the camera guy said. "Great. That's lunch."

"But I am already full!" Tabby said, smacking her lips and patting her belly.

"You ain't never full," one of the guys I didn't know said.

"Ah, you know me too well," she replied.

I watched Malloy approach her, speaking in a low voice as she unselfconsciously scrubbed between her legs with a colorful beach towel. She nodded agreeably and then walked away, motioning for him to follow. Malloy gestured for me to join him. I had noticed Dick Dallas circling me like a hungry shark so I hustled quickly over to Malloy.

"What's up?" I asked.

"She'll do it," Malloy replied. "She said she'll translate the note."

We followed Tabby over to the large bathroom and she waved us inside, locking the door behind us.

"Who is your little boy friend," Tabby asked, looking me up and down as she stripped off the stained rags of her cheerleader outfit.

"My nephew," Malloy said. "He got beat up by some punks, so he's staying with me for a while. He's okay."

Again that heart pounding stretch of seconds while I waited to be recognized. Tabby's electric blue eyes lingered on my face for a moment that felt like a century but then turned back to her own reflection in the mirror, pulling her fingers through her sticky red hair extensions.

"That's terrible," she said, peeling off her false eyelashes. "Well, let me see this note."

Malloy handed her the note and to his obvious dismay, she sat down on the toilet and had at it right in front of us, brow furrowed and fat lips moving while she read. Malloy took a step back and shot me a look. I just smirked. You gotta love Tabby. That girl has no shame.

"Okay," Tabby said, wincing with a pained grimace as she wiped. "You want I should write it down, what this says?"

"That'd be great," Malloy said, tearing a sheet of paper from a notebook and handing her a pen. "Thanks."

"I am happy to help Didi," Tabby said. She stood, taking the pen and flushing the toilet. "Because I don't believe any of this bullshit. Angel Dare is not a murderer. She couldn't do it, I know. Now, me. I could do it like that." She snapped her sparkle-nailed fingers. "Somebody does wrong to me, I do double back to them. That is the way where I come from. But I know Angel Dare, she has good heart. Maybe she is bitch to producers who don't respect her models or to the pushy jealous boyfriends that want to control the girls, but she is good person inside. And you, baby, you are good man to help her."

I looked away and my eye snagged on my own reflection. That stranger in the mirror. Was I really a good person? I wanted to kill Jesse and his boss, but maybe Tabby was right. Maybe I didn't have it in me.

Tabby bent down over the toilet, writing with her piece of notebook paper against the toilet tank. Her huge implants jiggled as she wrote, wrinkling like cheap plastic trash bags under her armpits. Malloy stood back beside me, eyes averted from Tabby's high-mileage ass. I looked over at the scatter of cheap make-up on the counter by the sink. Without even really knowing why, I put my hand over a glossy red lipstick and then swiftly pocketed it when no one was looking.

"Okay," Tabby announced, straightening up and handing the paper to Malloy. "I am finished."

"Thanks," Malloy said, scanning quickly over her translation.

"My pleasure, baby," she replied. "But this note. It is very bad what this girl writes. Very bad, but not so surprising, I am sad to say. These terrible things happen too much often to foreign girls, but tell me, what does this note has to do with Angel."

"That's what I intend to find out," Malloy said, folding the translation and the original together and stashing them in the pocket of his jacket. "One other thing. Do you know the girl who wrote this note? Romanian chick, goes by the name of Kimberly or maybe Lia? Did a series called *Naughty Teens*?"

"I had a aunt named Lia," Tabby said. "But she was a fat, religious woman with eight kids and more hair on her chin than I have on my pussy." She turned on the hot water in the shower. "I think maybe I heard of *Naughty Teens*. Amateur, right? Me, I don't get hired for the amateur shoots anymore." She grinned and hefted her implants. "Two big reasons."

"Well," Malloy said. "Thanks for your help. And keep

this to yourself, okay. At least until I can find Angel and sort this whole mess out."

"You have my word," Tabby said. "I hope you find the motherfuckers that do this to Angel."

About half an hour later, Malloy and I sat together in a booth at Bob's Big Boy on Riverside Drive in Burbank. I was feeling tired and surly and I had to piss. It never used to be a big deal, pissing. Now it was this source of major angst. I couldn't go in the ladies room and didn't want to go in the men's room, so I just sat there and held it. I was pretty damn sick of the whole business and from where I was sitting I didn't see any end in sight.

Malloy ate a burger. I tried to concentrate on Tabby's translation of Lia's letter while pushing uneaten chunks of fruit around on my plate.

Dear Lenuta,

Remember me, Lia Albu from the Saint Agnes Home for Orphan Girls? I am in terrible trouble with bad men. They bring me here to have job as nanny and then take my passport. They make me be prostitute and do porno to pay back for ticket but they claim so many expenses and I cannot get any money. They never leave me alone. They beat me and put drugs in me, but I am smart. I make this man Vukasin like me like a girlfriend, then I steal money and run away. Now I need your help, please, not for me but for my sister Ana. Remember little Ana? Before I run with money, I find out these bad men bring her too, at the end of this month the 27th. I read her name on a list and I know they lie to her like they lie to me. Please meet me in the food court of the Sherman Oaks Fashion Square Mall at noon on Monday. I can do nothing myself but I will give you money to buy Ana and five other girls, to save them from this hell that I have lived. If I call police the bad men will run and take Ana with them. This is only way. Please, Lenuta. I can trust no one else.

Lia

I set the letter aside and speared an anemic-looking cube of watermelon with my fork. I looked it over then put it back down uneaten. I wondered briefly why I had ordered this crummy fruit salad anyway. Honestly, there wasn't much point in sticking to my diet, what with everything that had happened and was still happening. Who's got time to fret over the size of your ass when you're busy trying to keep it out of jail?

"What do you know about Zandora's background?" Malloy asked around a mouthful of burger.

"She got married to an older American man through one of those mail-order bride services when she was just eighteen," I told him. "I know this'll come as a big shock, but she didn't really love the guy. She just wanted to get out of Bucharest and into sunny southern California."

"Shocking," Malloy agreed, sipping his coffee and shaking his head.

"When she got here, she stayed married just long enough to become a citizen and then decided the best way to ditch the boring old hubby was to get into porn. Amazingly, the guy hung in there for way longer than any of us expected. I guess he figured she'd get over it. She didn't and eventually he got over her. She got her divorce and he went back and got a new wife from a different country. Anyway she never mentioned that she was an orphan but she never talked about her family." I shrugged. "Hey, I'm not an orphan and I never talk about my family either."

"Why not?" Malloy asked. "You don't get along?"

"That's putting it mildly," I said.

"Because of the videos?" Malloy asked.

I shrugged.

"Nah," I said. "I mean, that too, but it started way before that. I figured if I was going to be branded as the Whore of Babylon anyway…" I sipped my weak, awful coffee. "I might as well get paid for it."

Malloy waited to see if I would say anything else. I didn't. I wasn't ready to open up that can of worms for him or for anybody. It was all ancient history and besides, there just wasn't any point in trying to explain to a man what it feels like to be the neighborhood slut, the girl with the bad reputation who lets boys do things to her and doesn't even try to get a ring.

Girls back home never could stand the fact that I was different. Before I had tits, I was just a misfit. An outcast troublemaker who liked to read and watch horror movies and thought Mary and Jesus and all the saints were just made up to make us behave in school. They teased me and made fun of me, but they didn't really give me much thought. Once the hormones kicked in, that's when I became a genuine threat. I wasn't just that I loved sex, it was the fact that I didn't use it as a bargaining chip. I didn't want to trade it for a house and a mess of kids,

I actually enjoyed it for its own sake, because it felt good. For that, the girls all hated me. Boys on the other hand, they loved me. That is until reality kicked in and they traded me in for a more sensible, wife-worthy model.

Me, I didn't want to be anybody's wife. I saw my own mother, drowning her regrets in gallon-bottle red wine and watching herself fade away to nothing, alone in the empty kitchen every single night, and I didn't want to be like her. I saw my older sister Denise go from a vibrant, intelligent young woman who wanted to travel and dreamed of becoming an opera singer to an exhausted, fat and shrewish mother whose entire world was about diapers and dishes and laundry while her husband stayed out all night screwing girls like me. My brothers' wives, my few friends and many enemies from high school, one after the other, the females around me sank into the tar of motherhood and debt and responsibility. The boys settled into dead end, blue-collar jobs and the girls raised their babies and waited for them to come home from the bars. Like victims in a slasher film, they all went down, one after another, until the only ones left standing were me and my best friend Stacy Cooney.

Stacy and I were the two biggest sluts in school. As fellow pariahs often do, we formed an immediate alliance. She was a redhead, a tiny freckled thing with mosquito-bite tits and a big mouth. Unlike me, she was a hard drinker from a long line of Irish drinkers and could put away more straight liquor in one night than most guys twice her size. If you measured her from the crown of her teased up mane of red Irish curls to the bottom of her spike-heeled boots, she was my height, around five seven.

Fresh out of the shower with bare feet, she was more like four eleven. Maybe 100 pounds, tops. She was my partner in crime. The first girl I ever kissed. She used to call me her getaway driver. We were like Siamese twins for the last year of high school and the two years that followed. We had some wild times, me and Stacy. Stacy loved guys in bands and there wasn't a venue in the state of Illinois where she couldn't get backstage. It had been her idea to hook up with an L.A. band and go to Hollywood to make dirty movies. Party with rock stars on the Sunset Strip, buy matching convertibles and never have to wear winter coats over our sexy outfits ever again. We had everything all planned out. A band from Los Angeles was coming through that June. We would take only one bag each, whatever money we had saved, and our best high-heeled boots. It was going to be a grand adventure. Then Stacy got knocked up.

She had no idea who the father was, but as cheerfully sinful as she had always been, she was genuinely terrified of going to hell if she had an abortion. Within a week of the failed pregnancy test, she had some sap all set to marry her and take care of the kid. All our foolish dreams meant nothing now that there was a baby to think about. Something about the resigned look on her face when she told me it was best if we didn't hang out anymore hurt worse than any guy who'd ever dumped me.

I packed my things. I had to get out, before having a baby and settling down into the tar started sounding like a good idea to me, too.

I went to that concert alone and I got myself backstage. I threw everything in my arsenal at the handsome singer and he took the bait even though I knew he could see the hook. He was a good lover and he was gracious enough to let me hitch a ride with the band back to Los Angeles. I won't kiss and tell, but that band went on to become hugely famous, then widely reviled and ridiculed, and then famous again. The singer and I stayed in touch; we're still good friends. Not Stacy. I haven't heard from her since the day she told me we couldn't hang out anymore. Come to think of it, her failed pregnancy test would now be old enough to do porn.

"You done?" Malloy asked, pulling me gently back into the present.

I looked down at the remains of my fruit salad.

"Yeah," I said.

"Right," Malloy said, pulling out his wallet and signaling the waitress.

That reminded me of something I'd meant to do since I woke up in Ulka's dungeon. Something that would make me feel just a tiny bit less dependent on Malloy. Something that would make me feel a little more like me again.

I'd kept a storage locker on Haskell and Roscoe by the Budweiser plant ever since the Northridge earthquake back in '94. I had just bought my house the year before and luckily it didn't suffer any major damage, but that quake scared the piss out of me. Hence, this storage locker. A secret stash of just-in-case that no one knew about but me. Even though I'd had no idea anything like this could ever happen, I'd still had it in my head that I needed the place to be a secret, so I'd rented it under a fake name. That was back when it was still easy to do that kind of thing, before the whole 9/11 business. I paid yearly in cash and never caused any trouble. Kept a fat combination lock on it so there was no key to lose. Just in case.

Inside the storage locker was exactly the sort of junk you expect to find in storage lockers. A few boxes. Some books. An old lamp. A trio of vintage hats. A blocky toy robot that used to light up but didn't anymore. An ugly, floral-print easy chair. Nothing to make a casual observer look twice. Nothing boost-worthy. But the boxes, marked with red Sharpie letters that read things like "Hot Rollers," "Kitchen" and "Photos," actually contained bottled water, military MRE rations, a Swiss army knife, a flashlight, extra batteries, a first aid kit and several rolls of toilet paper.

If you actually sat in that ugly chair, you'd find it extremely uncomfortable. The chair's lumpy seat cushion had a zippered cover that could be removed for cleaning. The zipper was rusty and cantankerous but when you unzipped it, you would find several items stuffed in with the crumbling yellow foam rubber. First, a Saran-wrapped stack of cash adding up to two grand. Enough to smooth things out in a emergency where bank access was impossible, but not more than I could afford to lose if anything should happen to compromise this place. Then, if you reached in deeper, you'd encounter a more recent, post-9/11 addition: a scruffy old Smith and Wesson .40 caliber pistol that wasn't nearly as nice as my stolen Sig and about which I knew very little other than a disreputable acquaintance's assurance that it was untraceable. I had never fired it. I cleaned and oiled it when I came to rotate out the water, batteries or food but in my mind it was really nothing but another piece of my just-in-case juju. I had been thinking earthquake, riots, terrorists. Never in a million years did I imagine that I would be planning on using that gun to commit premeditated murder.

Because when you get right down to it, that's what this was all about, wasn't it? I mean, sure, I was going along with Malloy on this whole Nancy Drew song and dance, snooping around and trying to put the pieces together to figure out what the hell was going on, but what I was really doing was biding my time until the time came to even the score. I didn't want to find myself face to face with Jesse or his boss without a way to make them pay for what they did to me.

I pulled out the box of bullets I had also stuffed into the chair cushion and carefully loaded the unfamiliar clip. I didn't feel comfortable with the loaded gun in any of my pockets or down the waistband of my pants like some TV gangster, so I dug out a nylon duffel bag from the clutter and put the pistol, the bullets and the cash into one of its interior zippered pockets.

As I turned to go, I found my gaze traveling over the assortment of dusty items around me. It was just a bunch of useless junk, bought at thrift stores as set dressing to cover up the real purpose of the locker, but I realized in that moment that those things were the only personal things I owned that I still had free access to. I picked up the little robot with a hollow kind of feeling in my stomach. It was old, but not old enough to be collectable.

Just some cheap plastic Korean thing with a squat boxy body and stubby square arms and legs. The colored lights in its chest were dark and useless and the shiny silver coating on the gray plastic was starting to peel around the joints. I remembered buying that robot at the Salvation Army store for a dollar. Now this cheap broken robot some kid didn't want anymore was pretty much all I had left. Before I could think too much about it, I stuck the little robot in my duffel bag and got the hell out of there. I didn't tell Malloy about the robot. Or the gun.

16.

What came next was something I had been dreading, for a complex variety of reasons. Malloy and I went back and forth over the issue of the security tapes in the Daring Angels building on Vesper. In the end we decided that there was no way to get around me going with him. He knew a lot of my girls, but not all of them. I needed to be the one to see the tape and ID the people who'd come and gone in the seven hours between when Lia left and when I did. I had been more than willing to let the whole thing slide and concentrate on finding Lia but Malloy seemed hell-bent on finding that damn briefcase.

"You can bet everyone's gonna be keeping an eye on that place," Malloy said. "Cops and crooks. Now I'm good with the former so far, but not so much with the latter. The guy who got away in Vegas clearly hasn't figured out who I am yet because we haven't had any visitors at my place but if he's the one they have on the Vesper Avenue location there's gonna be trouble."

I nodded, wordless. The familiar lowbrow landscape of Van Nuys Boulevard scrolled by outside the passenger window, as distant and meaningless as a swimmy rear projection in a old black and white movie. I must have driven up and down this street a thousand times, four days a week for nine years. Now it felt sort of like watching home movies from when I was a kid, or watching my first scene with Marco Pole. It felt unreal.

Malloy made the right turn onto Archwood, just past Vanowen and I felt a wash of anxiety. He passed the Vesper Avenue building twice, scoping the block. Looking for surveillance, I supposed, but I just couldn't seem to make myself concentrate. I was lost in the middle of this sudden, vicious gang rape of memories. The past was a bully that day and there were so many memories connected to that place, so much personal history.

When I started Daring Angels back in 1997, I had been doing dirty videos for nine years. I was tired of the on-camera grind and I had this strange, almost superstitious fear of that tenth year that I still can't quite explain. I guess I didn't want to spend a full decade of my life making ooh-baby in front of a camera. For the last couple of years before I retired, so many younger women had come to me, asking for advice, for backup, for help navigating the shark-infested waters of the smut racket. Eventually my friends started joking that I ought to charge for my advice. As that dreaded tenth year loomed closer and closer, I stopped laughing and started planning.

I remembered going to look at the hot, echoey space that would eventually be the Daring Angels office, sneezing from the construction dust and wondering if I was making a big mistake. See, I wanted out, but I couldn't stand to leave the business altogether. After all, I was a star. A big name. Angel Dare. I just couldn't bear to give that up. Sure, the porn industry can be infuriating, but in its own brash and vulgar way it's kind of like a big, dysfunctional family. A lot of women wound up feeling used by the porn industry, but they were just the ones who never figured out how to use it right back.

Starting up Daring Angels, I was banking on the idea

that girls in the business needed a positive alternative to the boyfriend/managers, the suitcase pimps and the predatory, mostly male-run talent agencies. They needed a female-owned and -operated agency that treated the girls with respect, that had their backs and made sure that they didn't get eaten alive and spat back out in under a year. I had a solid business plan, an electronic Rolodex to die for and Didi as my right-hand woman. I had a modest roster of four fresh, gorgeous girls and I even had cute business cards featuring a sexy, winking angel drawn by a famous comic book artist I had been banging at the time. I felt ready to take on the world.

That first year was hard. The second was harder. I fucked up a lot, lost money and learned some painful lessons. But by the third year, I had my shit down. I had a Web site up and running and was working to add a special members-only area with original content featuring the Daring Angels girls. I was doing recruiting trips out to strip clubs in bumfuck nowheresville, sniffing out fresh talent anywhere I could find it. I'd never made a mint off Daring Angels, but combined with interest from my investments, I managed to make a pretty comfortable living. Until all this.

"Looks clear," Malloy told me, pulling into a free slot on the other side of Archwood. "I can't believe it, but the place looks pretty much deserted." He killed the ignition. "Still, stay close."

I got out of the car, hoisted my duffel on my shoulder and made my legs carry me toward the place that used to be my office. My mind brushed briefly against a murky, buried question about the ultimate fate of Daring Angels and flinched away, as if it had touched something repulsive. I just couldn't handle speculation on the future right then. All I needed was to get through this moment. I would worry about the future...well...in the future.

The building was nondescript and so familiar that I barely saw it. Now that I was on the outside of my old life looking in, every detail seemed weirdly intensified. The dried-blood-maroon-and-bone-white paint job. The ugly, functional architecture, everything featureless and rectangular. Long, uninviting balconies along the building's Archwood flank, the one on the first floor fenced in like a zoo cage. My office didn't have a balcony so my rent was two hundred dollars cheaper and you had to go downstairs and outside if you wanted to smoke.

Inside the lobby, beside the staircase leading up to the upper floors, was a security station. Nothing but a cheap metal desk with a guy in a uniform behind it.

The security guard was a new kid I'd never seen before. The usual guy had been a thick, oily walrus of a man with a white pushbroom mustache and a lascivious wink for any female who entered the building. This new kid was lanky and Mexican and afflicted with a plague of acne so juicy and virulent that it looked almost radioactive. Beneath the zits lurked a handsome, square-jawed face and you could see that he would have a hard, sexy tough-guy look about him once he did a little growing up and his overzealous hormones finally gave it a rest. He was sitting behind the crummy little desk reading a dense legal textbook that he did not bother to put down when we approached him. His nametag said CAMMAROTA.

"Hey," Malloy said.

"Hey," the kid replied over the top of his book with a great show of sullen indifference.

"I'm investigating the disappearance of Angel Dare." Malloy said. He indicated the dusty camera up above the kid's head. "I was wondering if it might be possible to take a look at the security tapes from last Friday."

"You a cop?" the kid asked, finally looking up at Malloy. His dark eyes were sharp under the mask of acne.

"Used to be," Malloy said. "I'm just looking into the matter for a private party."

"Angel Dare, that's the porno chick, huh?" the kid asked, warming to the topic. "The one on the news who shot that guy."

"Right," Malloy said.

I had been standing slightly behind Malloy, keeping a low profile. It wasn't until that kid mentioned me that I started to feel like I had big arrows flashing over my head. Like the whole dressed-up-like-a-boy business couldn't fool a blind man. In spite of that unshakable feeling, the kid didn't even look at me. He was just talking about some chick on TV.

"That's messed up," the kid said.

"Right," Malloy said again. "How about those tapes?"

The kid put the book down and stood.

"Come on," the kid said, looking around. "I'm not supposed to leave the station, but…"

We followed him down a narrow first floor hallway that I had never noticed before. At the end of the hall was a door with no number. The Mexican kid opened the door with a key on a ring that extended out from his belt on a spring-loaded black cord. Inside was a closet-sized office cluttered with cleaning products and plastic file boxes.

"They only keep the tapes for ten days," the kid said, pulling a plastic crate down from a high shelf. "Then they recycle them. It's a good thing you didn't wait too long to ask about it. Do you think there could be, like, clues or something on the tape?"

"Could be," Malloy said.

The kid frowned into the box and Malloy frowned too.

"What?" Malloy asked.

"I hate to tell you this," the kid said. "But I think last Friday is missing."

"What do you mean, missing?" Malloy asked, taking the box from the kid's arms and sifting efficiently through the contents. "Son of a bitch."

"Where..." I paused and cleared my throat, struggling to deepen my voice as best I could. "Where's the regular guy?"

"I don't know," the kid said shrugging. "I just started this job today."

Malloy shot me a look.

"Okay, kid," Malloy said. "Thanks anyway."

"You think somebody took it?" the kid asked.

"Probably," Malloy said, shrugging like it didn't matter.

"Maybe the cops have it," the kid offered helpfully. "Or maybe somebody broke in and stole it. Like maybe that porno chick snuck in here in the middle of the night so that she could...I don't know, hide some evidence or something like that."

Malloy nodded as if he was seriously considering the

kid's theory. I supposed I ought to have been pissed at all this speculation about me, but it seemed so irrelevant, like a discussion of a movie I'd never seen. Like they really were just talking about some chick on TV.

We left Cammarota in the back room and hustled back out to the lobby. As Malloy held the glass door open for me to pass, he leaned in and hissed in my ear.

"You don't know me," he said. "Walk down to Victory and I'll meet you."

I turned left out the door and started walking quickly, but not too quickly, away. Over my shoulder I heard a man's voice call Malloy's name, but I didn't want to risk a backward glance.

I turned south on Vesper Avenue, the whole back of my body clenched and cringing as if expecting a bullet. My buzzcut scalp felt painfully vulnerable. I was dying to know what the hell was going on back there, but I didn't want to chance being recognized. I couldn't hear anything but the sounds of the street. Cars, distant music, a hedge trimmer. I reached Victory Boulevard much sooner than I meant to and stood there on the corner by the 7-Eleven, feeling stupid and unsure. I turned and looked up at the mural on the side of the Family Medical Center building next door. I'd seen that mural about a million times, but I'd never actually paid attention. It showed three guys standing on top of the planet Earth, reaching for a sort of three-way high five. One guy was wearing a winter hat and scarf. The other two were in t-shirts. I had no idea who those guys were supposed to be.

I couldn't stop myself from looking back toward my building but I was too far away and couldn't see anything at all. I had no idea where Malloy was. Cars passed and people passed and I was hit with a sudden terror that I was really totally alone. Disconnected. No home, no car, no real identity anymore. Nowhere to go but jail. I pressed my body against the sooty skin of the 7-Eleven building, feeling like I needed to hold on to something solid or else I would just disintegrate or tumble up into the smoggy yellow sky.

Following swiftly on the heels of that fear was a kind of slinking guilt. I kept on telling myself not to become dependent on Malloy, and yet the second he was out of my sight I panicked like a little kid lost in the supermarket. I had money. I could find a motel that didn't require a credit card and hole up. Find a way to contact Didi. She would know where to find Jesse. I could make Jesse tell me where I could find his boss, that bland-faced fucker who was clearly responsible for everything that had been done to me. I didn't need a goddamn babysitter.

I unzipped my duffel and pulled out the little robot. I don't know what I was hoping for. Maybe I thought that holding that talisman from my former life would calm and center me somehow. In the end it just made me feel self-conscious and silly, like some loony homeless person you would cross the street to avoid. Next thing I knew I'd be saving my pee in glass jars and pushing a shopping cart.

"Angel," Malloy said, hand on my shoulder, and I jumped like he had goosed me, dropping the little robot.

Malloy deftly caught the robot before it could smash on the concrete. I turned back to him and wrapped my arms around myself.

"Christ," I said. "You scared the shit out of me."

Malloy looked down at the robot and up at me, then

handed it back to me without comment. I stuck the robot back into my bag, feeling more foolish than ever.

"What happened?" I asked.

"It was Erlichman, one of those young hard-ons that caught your case," Malloy said. "Wanted to know what I was doing snooping around your office."

"What did you tell him?" I asked, following Malloy as he turned and headed east on Victory. The sun was beating down on my newly shorn scalp, giving me a nasty headache.

"I told him what he already knew," Malloy said. "That Didi paid me to look into your disappearance. I asked about the tape too. Erlichman doesn't have it, so I'm guessing either the guy from Vegas or his boss has got it. They'll be paying a visit to everyone that visited your office that day."

"Shit," I said, trying to shake the image of Zandora lying dead in her cotton panties and focus on remembering who all had been into the office on the last day of my former life. "I remember several of the girls came by and at least one director that I can think of."

"Erlichman is gone," Malloy said. "Think it would help jog your memory to go back up to your office?"

I shivered. Going back up into my office was the last thing on earth I wanted to do. I shrugged, looking away.

We circled the block and came around to the back of the building. No one in sight. I trudged reluctantly behind Malloy as he slipped in and headed up the steps to the second floor, nodding to the kid behind the guard desk. I didn't want to do this. Didn't want to view the corpse of my old life. It didn't look like Malloy was going to give me a choice.

I couldn't have prepared myself for that any more than I could have prepared for the first time I saw my beat-up face in the mirror. The lock was busted and the door hung ajar behind yellow police tape. Malloy pushed through the tape and led me into the frozen crime scene my former life had become.

The place was trashed. Didi's desk was a cluttered mess of emptied drawers and rifled files. Her computer was gone. The comfy purple chairs Didi and I had picked out had been shoved together in one corner. The carafe for my coffee pot lay broken on the carpet. The door to my own office was closed, and I found I was weirdly grateful for that.

"Okay," Malloy said, heading toward the bathroom door. "You say the girl definitely had the briefcase when she went into the bathroom, right?"

I nodded, unable to squeeze words past the hot lump in my throat.

"She could have taken the case with her out the window," Malloy said, pushing the bathroom door open. Lia's expensive heels were still on the floor by the toilet. "Maybe she ditched it somewhere right outside, in a dumpster or something like that, since the boss told you she 'left without it.' But I get the feeling she didn't take it with her. I think it had to be stashed here somewhere. Clearly the boss thought the same thing, only his men didn't find it. Someone else did. So where could she have hidden it?"

I shrugged and watched in a numb daze while Malloy searched the tiny bathroom. It was much too small for anyone to hide anything. Malloy stood on the closed lid of the toilet, reaching up toward the low, acoustic tile ceiling, lifting each tile one by one. My heart skipped as something black clattered down and bounced off the toilet tank to land on the floor by the sink. It wasn't the briefcase but as soon as I realized what it was, I saw with forehead-slapping clarity exactly what had happened. I knew who had the briefcase.

17.

The black object lying on the bathroom floor was a sleek, spike-heeled calfskin boot by Manolo Blahnik. Those boots, I had been informed by a very huffy director, cost over twelve hundred dollars and she would not be inclined to press charges if they were simply returned, no questions asked. The shoot had been for Top Notch and the girl who had been fucked in those twelve hundred dollar boots was Roxette DuMonde.

Roxette was not a bad kid, but she had a magpie's eye and a compulsion for nicking shiny things. She was the black sheep child of New York high society and had been a fashion model in her early teens. I guess her rich but distant daddy didn't hug her enough when she was growing up, because she rapidly tumbled from *Vogue* to *Penthouse* to porn and bottomed out at twenty, declared clinically dead for nearly two minutes after an overdose of crystal meth. After she got clean, she came to me. I was very leery of taking on a girl with a drug problem, reformed or not, but Roxette was just that gorgeous. Directors and fans could not get enough of her. She looked kind of like a bratty, juvenile delinquent version of Linda Evangelista. Terrifyingly flawless, yet she was willing to do almost anything on camera. Even before I had officially agreed to take her on, I was getting phone calls from guys who wanted to book her, just on the rumor that she might be getting back into the business.

It was crazy, but I guess eventually the dollar signs won out over any doubts or misgivings. We had the biggest traffic spike in the history of our Web site the day I uploaded the first set of exclusive new Roxette photos.

She'd been with me for a little over a year and had never fallen off the wagon like I feared, but she…borrowed things. It seemed to happen all the time. Never anything of real value, just trinkets mostly. She stole gaudy baubles, stockings and lipsticks from the other girls. She pinched figurines, silver forks and fancy coasters from the locations where she did shoots. She had plenty of money from her bazillionaire parents and from all the top-drawer shoots and feature tours she did, so it's not like she needed the things she took. Whenever she was confronted, she would just arrange her famous mouth into its signature sexy pout and somehow she would be forgiven. The scary-pretty ones always were able to get away with murder.

But those boots were a different story. They were not cheap trinkets, they were pricey designer items that Celestine, the dragon lady director in charge of Roxette's last shoot, had instantly missed. I had Didi call Roxette and tell her to come into the office at 9AM sharp. I told Celestine ten, since I knew I could count on Roxette to be at least an hour late. When Roxette showed up lugging her enormous gig bag and drinking iced green tea from a trendy coffee bar, she saw Celestine sitting beside my desk and blanched. She asked to go to the bathroom first and I let her. She took her bag with her.

When she came out she was all big-eyed and cute. She seemed totally baffled, denied having the boots and offered to let Celestine search her bag. She told Celestine she didn't know what possibly could have happened to the boots after she took them off, but offered to do an extra set of stills for the Top Notch website to smooth over any hard feelings. Like everyone always did, Celestine somehow went from pissed off and ready to call the police to hugging Roxette and apologizing for the accusation. I just shrugged and let it go. What else could I do?

But clearly Roxette had taken the boots. She must have stashed them under the acoustic tile in the bathroom ceiling right before the meeting with Celestine. I also remembered how Roxette had come back just after the weird business with Lia, saying she had been doing some errands nearby and had to pee really bad. She'd claimed she was recovering from yet another urinary infection and wasn't able to hold it until she got back to her Malibu condo. Anyone who's ever been in the industry knows those kinds of female troubles all too well, plus she'd looked so cute with her knees pressed together like a squirming child. She'd still had that big gig bag with her and lugged it into the bathroom again, using it to prop the broken door closed. In retrospect, I figured she'd been planning to retrieve the boots, but instead, she'd found a mysterious briefcase. Curious magpie that she was, she'd forgotten all about the boots and snagged the case instead, stashing it inside the roomy gig bag.

I made Malloy get the other boot out from under the ceiling tile and put the pair into my own duffel bag. I mean, hey, Celestine had already written them off, and it seemed a shame to leave such expensive designer boots just lying there on the bathroom floor. Especially since Roxette and I have the same size feet.

I filled Malloy in on the way back to his car. I tried phoning Roxette, but didn't get an answer and didn't want to leave a message. She wouldn't be too hard to find. I knew her address, the gym where she worked out and all her favorite clubs. The only thing we really needed to worry about was that she might have broken open the lock on the case and gone hog-wild with the money inside. Malloy seemed to think that if we had the money, we would have a bargaining chip, a way to draw out the boss and make him come to us. Me, I figured that money was mine. Compensation for the wholesale destruction of my life. The world's highest asshole tax.

Faced with another long night on Malloy's sofa, I decided to spring for some over-the-counter sleeping pills along with the Sweet'N Low, green grapes and salted almonds I picked up for myself at the Ralph's on the way back to Burbank. I also impulse-bought a pretty blue coffee mug, because it felt inexplicably important to have my own cup. Money might not buy happiness, but I'll tell you what, it doesn't hurt.

In the end, I couldn't take the sleeping pills after all. I just sat there staring at the Good Housekeeping Seal of Approval on the Sominex label, wondering what would happen if bad guys with guns showed up in the middle of the night and I couldn't wake up.

Eventually, morning came instead of bad guys. That was the thing about mornings. No matter how fucked up your life got, how deep and black your despair, how sure you were that you just couldn't take another second of this shit, morning just kept on coming. Over and over. Morning didn't give a damn about your little drama.

Morning brought Malloy from his bedroom lair again, just like the day before. He looked the same as ever. I showered while he made coffee and read the paper. Ozzy and fucking Harriet. If you squinted, it all seemed almost normal. Except for the part about me being an ex-porn star dressed up like a boy, wanted by the cops and on the run from the psycho ringleader of some kind of prostitution slavery racket who'd tried to have me killed once and wanted to finish the job. Noon seemed to take forever to show up.

When it was finally time to head over to the mall in Sherman Oaks and see if Lia would be there at the hour specified in her note to Zandora, I quickly wrapped my tits and waist and put in the blue contacts. It had been so nice to just relax without all those sweaty uncomfortable mummy bandages. As we were headed out the door, I decided at the last minute to wash out my new blue cup, wrap it in my last two t-shirts and stick it in the duffel bag with the little robot and the boots. I couldn't shake this powerful need to keep my meager possessions with me at all times. Of course, I could get into serious trouble for bringing a loaded gun to the mall, but hey, at this point that was the least of the reasons why I might be arrested. I didn't worry all that much about it.

18.

What can I say about the Sherman Oaks Fashion Square mall? You've been to any mall in America, you don't need me to describe the place. Stores. Shoppers. The American consumer dream all spread out and waiting, available for a price. Everything your sheep-like heart has been trained to desire. I hate malls. They're like strip clubs for women. All tease and sparkle and the empty promise that if you just drop enough cash, somehow you'll be fulfilled. The slick, shameless, never-ending hustle of a shopping mall makes places like Eye Candy look downright charitable by comparison. When I need to buy stuff, I'd much rather shop online. That way I don't have to battle my way through all those lonely, desperate, retail-therapy junkies. Nothing more depressing than watching these skinny, manic women digging their own graves with a credit card while their bored husbands furtively eye my assets, trying to figure out if I really am Angel Dare or just look like her. The only kind of store I really love to browse in is a hardware store. I'm a compulsive fixer-upper, always on the lookout for new things for my house. At least I used to be. I have no idea what I am now.

Our destination was the food court and at that weekday lunch hour it was packed with cubicle drones wearing sensible shoes and laminated IDs around their necks. The ring of fast food options represented all the usual franchise suspects. Chinese, Italian, American, Middle Eastern. Ostensible variety that was really all the same school lunch food under different-flavored sauces.

Still, as much as I might hate malls, you had to admit Lia had made a smart choice for a meeting place. It was public, patrolled by security guards and packed with potential witnesses. I wondered how a girl who was essentially a captive sex slave from another country knew about this mall, but remembering her note claiming to have gotten one guy to "like her like a girlfriend" made me remember her expensive hair and nails. Her fancy heels. I pictured her working on her erstwhile beau to take her shopping. Batting her eyelashes and talking of lingerie and sexy shoes and all the while taking mental notes, memorizing everything. That girls had brains, I'd give her that. Brains and balls.

Malloy wanted us to move through the mall separately. Close but not obviously together.

"That way," Malloy told me as he had parked the car up on a high, nearly deserted level of the parking structure, "if I get recognized, you won't. We don't know if your pal from Vegas got the note or information about its contents out of Zandora before we showed up or not. No point taking unnecessary chances."

I opened the make-up mirror inside the visor on the passenger side and snuck a quick glance at the reflected image of that blond guy, Daniel. Imagining I was someone else made mirrors less of an ordeal.

The fading bruises around my eyes made the new blue contacts look lurid and too bright. The white tape had peeled off my nose in the shower that morning but some black sticky adhesive gunk was left behind and I couldn't get it off because it hurt to scrub too hard. I ran a hand over the bleachy yellow buzz cut. I wouldn't recognize me.

We left the car and headed down into the mall. I tailed Malloy past the Gap, past the Body Shop, threading through the lunchtime crowd in his wake until we reached the abovementioned food court.

I stationed myself by a smoothie stand where I had a decent view of the whole court and several exits. Every skinny blonde that passed made my heart twist under my ribs but none of them were Lia. Noon came and went without incident.

I watched Malloy lingering by the Sbarro and then without meeting my eyes he made a tight little gesture with his chin toward the stairs that led up to a second-level seating area. Unsure if he meant for me to follow him or not, I watched him head up, out of sight. Then, less than ten seconds later, he was heading back down. I could read the tension under his casual stroll and I wasn't all that surprised when I spotted the weasel, my pal from Vegas, coming down the steps behind him.

I turned away, pretending to study the smoothie menu while watching Malloy out of the corner of my eye. He walked right past me and went into the bookstore on my left. I had no idea what he was doing. Apparently, neither did the weasel, but he followed Malloy into the store anyway.

I knew nothing could happen here in the mall, in full view of the security guards and all these civilians, but I also figured the weasel would follow us up through the parking structure and in that big hollow empty space it would be a whole different story.

Malloy and I had agreed that if anything went wrong

in the mall, I was supposed to get the hell out and catch a bus back to his place. He had given me a spare key and when he'd slipped it into my hip pocket, I'd felt almost like we were dating or something. I had spent more solid back-to-back time with Malloy than with anyone else since I'd moved out of my parents' house back in Chicago, yet we were not sleeping together. It felt so strange, unnatural somehow.

Watching Malloy browsing through the bookstore like there wasn't a homicidal scumbag following him around, I wondered if now wasn't a good time to bug out. Before I could decide one way or the other, I saw Malloy stumble and bump into the weasel, slapping his shoulder and smiling in that same dumb, friendly manner he had when he went into Eye Candy. I watched with baffled amazement, squinting and trying to figure out what the hell he was doing.

After his collision with the weasel, Malloy made his roundabout way out of the store. When the weasel followed, the shoplifting alarm went off.

Security guards immediately confronted the weasel and, after much protest from him, one of the guards pulled a small gilt-edged gift book from his jacket pocket. Some cheesy little thing full of uplifting quotes and photos of kittens, the kind of thing that you get as a gift from your grandmother and never read. Chicken Soup for the Homicidal Scumbag's Soul.

Malloy passed by me and whispered out of the corner of his mouth.

"Car," he said.

Then he was gone.

The weasel was being escorted out of the mall while

shouting angrily into his cell phone. I looked back up at the smoothie menu as if deciding between the Berry-licious VitaWhip or the Banana Mango Fandango. The busty, cow-eyed brunette behind the counter suddenly turned to me with an expression of startled panic, as if she'd only just noticed me even though I'd been standing there for several minutes. Her hair was chopped into one of those weird new mullety, cowlicky bowl-cuts and she had a ring through her lower lip that looked painfully infected. She grimaced and recited her upbeat franchise-robot script with a clenched and desperate tone.

"Good afternoon, sir, and welcome to Nutra-Freeze Healthy Smoothie Paradise. Can I take your order?"

Sir. God that was weird. I waited until the weasel made like Elvis and left the building, then I shook my head at the smoothie girl.

"I…uh…changed my mind," I told her.

She looked painfully relived. I thought, not unkindly, that with an impressive natural rack like hers, she'd do better to ditch the ugly orange Nutra-Freeze tunic and get into porn. That thought made me think of Sam. Thinking of Sam hurt and so I forced myself to think of getting the hell out of there.

I hustled back the way I came and headed for the parking structure. As I went, every single person I passed seemed leering and sinister. Teenage boys. Moms with strollers. Mall-walking grannies. They all looked like axe murderers to me. Paranoia notwithstanding, I somehow found my way back to the level where Malloy had parked the car.

I could hear a terse, stifled rhythm of punches and grunts coming from the opposite side of Malloy's SUV and my blood went cold. I stood there for a heartbeat or two, dumb and frozen like a rabbit in the headlights. Then, on a split-second impulse, I headed diagonally away from Malloy's car and over toward the only other vehicle parked on that level, a green minivan.

Standing by the minivan, fumbling through my pockets in a lame-ass pantomime of looking for keys I didn't have, I risked a peek back toward Malloy's car. I saw Malloy in a fierce, sloppy scuffle with a guy who was a little shorter than him but much thicker. The shorter guy looked like he was getting the upper hand over Malloy. There was blood on Malloy's flushed face and on the oily concrete at their feet. That's when I simultaneously realized two things. First, that the guy fighting with Malloy was the rhino—the guy who'd shot Sam in the knee. Second, that I had a loaded gun in my duffel bag.

19.

My first instinct was pure and unequivocal. Kill the son of a bitch. I knew in my gut that he had been the one who put the two bullets in the back of Sam's head.

But he and Malloy were close as lovers, moving erratically in every direction. I'm not a bad shot. I can hit pretty close to the middle of the paper guy more than half the time at the calm, empty shooting range. But in a situation like this, with my hands shaking, an unfamiliar gun and Malloy right there…well, I just didn't want to take any chances.

I put my hand inside the duffel bag and unzipped the inner pocket, closing my fingers around the cold weight of the pistol's nubby, ergonomic grip. I fumbled along the length of the barrel, hunting for the safety and feeling like my heart was going to burst inside my chest.

I wanted to shout something tough and manly like *Freeze, motherfucker, or I'll blow your balls off!* In the end I just pointed the gun and yelled, "Hey!"

The rhino and Malloy both turned toward my voice. There was no recognition in the rhino's eyes as he sized up this fey blond boy holding a gun. Then, almost before I could register what was happening, Malloy took advantage of the unexpected distraction to let the guy have it hard, right on the button. The rhino spun and crumpled to the concrete.

I rushed to Malloy's side, looking up into his bloody face.

"You okay?" I asked.

"You should see the other guy," he replied with that stingy rind of a smile on his bruised lips. He opened the driver's side door. "Let's get the hell out of here before any more of them show up."

I was about to go around to the passenger side and get in the car when I looked down at the rhino. He was unconscious, face down on the concrete and making a sort of snoring sound, arms and legs twitching like a dog chasing dream rabbits. Without even realizing I was doing it, I raised the gun and aimed it directly at the back of his head. My whole body felt cold and numb.

"Angel," Malloy said, putting a hand on my shoulder.

I shook him off and centered my aim again. I thought of Sam, of Georgie and all the shoots we did together. The fresh potato salad she always made and the time Sam put that strap-on dildo around his forehead and ran around the set claiming to be a unicorn looking to put his head in a virgin's lap. I dropped down on one knee beside the man who'd killed him and pressed the snout of the gun against the curve of the fucker's skull.

"Think for a second, Angel," Malloy asked quietly. "Are you sure this is what you want?"

I could hear the sound of Malloy's voice, but somehow it didn't seem to relate to me. All I could hear was that scream, that horrible high-pitched, almost child-like scream that had torn up out of Sam's throat when the rhino shot him in the knee. The only thing I was sure of was this kind of delirious, narcotic fury that gripped me and wouldn't let me go. I pulled the trigger.

The rhino was dead before I could put a second hole alongside the first, but I felt I needed to do it anyway, for Sam. The pistol's kick resonated endlessly along the long bones of my arm and my unprotected ears rang and then Malloy was grabbing me, hustling me roughly into the car and peeling out.

"Give me the gun," he said as he hung a sharp turn onto Moorpark.

I let him pry my fingers gently off the pistol's grip and then stash the gun under his seat.

I felt cold and muffled, as if I were underwater. The familiar, franchise-laden Valley landscape seemed hyper-detailed and implausible, like something drawn by a comic book artist on speed, but my own inner landscape was blurry and unclear.

If I'd been unsure how to feel about Malloy after witnessing what he had done to that thug in Vegas, how was I supposed to feel about myself now? That guy in Vegas had been trying to kill Malloy. Malloy was simply defending himself, even if he ultimately went too far. Me, I had shot and killed an unconscious man. Sure, he was trying to hurt Malloy, maybe kill him. He had shot Sam in the knee right in front of me, if not killed him, too. But the guy had been out like a baby when I'd shot him. What sort of person did that make me?

As if reading my mind, Malloy arched a silver eyebrow at me.

"Guess I was wrong about you," he said.

I remembered Malloy saying that he thought I wasn't the cold-blooded execution type. Tabby had said basically the same thing. Were they wrong? Had the events of the last few crazy days changed who I was or just allowed me to finally become who I had been all along?

There was something different in Malloy's guarded eyes when he looked at me now. I couldn't tell if it was admiration or wariness.

"Pull over," I hissed, breaking eye contact and clutching the dashboard as I was broadsided by a brutal wave of nausea.

I barely shouldered open the door in time to puke violently into the leafy gutter just before the corner of Riverside and Van Noord.

20.

Malloy waited out my bout of dry heaves. I felt fairly close either to passing out or turning inside out when I finally slammed the door, leaned back and rested my pounding head against the seat.

"It's no big deal," Malloy said, putting the car in gear and pulling back out into traffic. "Lots of guys puke the first time."

He reached under his seat and for a crazy second, I though he was going to pull out the gun. Instead, he came up with an unopened bottle of water and offered it to me without taking his eyes off the road. I accepted the water gratefully and took a deep swig. It was warm as tea, but I needed it.

"I was thirty," Malloy told me as we waited at a red light. "It was two days after my birthday. I was still a rookie back then. Got a kinda late start on the job."

He stuck a cigarette in the corner of his mouth and punched the dashboard lighter. The light changed and he hit the gas.

"Anyway," he continued, unlit cigarette bouncing as he spoke. "My partner and me, we got a call that this crackhead left her newborn baby in the toilet at a Carl's Jr. Left it in there just like you'd leave a dump." He shook his head. "We found her right around the corner, sitting on the ground, hitting the pipe like nothing happened. She was still bleeding down her legs. When my partner confronted her, she acted like she didn't hear him. Then when he took a step closer, she pulled out this knife. I don't mean some kind of pocketknife, I mean a big old kitchen knife like the kind on TV that cuts through tin cans. She stuck that knife right in Laimert's calf. So I shot her."

The lighter popped out. Malloy took it out and touched it to the end of his cigarette.

"I thought I was OK about it at first. I mean she was just a skinny little thing, barely more than a kid, but she was out of her fucking mind. She drowned her own baby in a dirty toilet and stabbed a cop. She had it coming, no doubt about it. But two hours later I was typing up some paperwork and all of a sudden, I saw her again, lying there on her side, and I puked right on the typewriter."

I looked up at Malloy. I was so surprised by this unexpected soliloquy that I didn't know what to say. Lalo Malloy, spontaneously sharing an intimate anecdote. With me. Something subtle and strange had happened between us. I had no idea what to make of it.

I looked out the window. Sherman Oaks became Valley Village and then North Hollywood as we zigzagged back toward Malloy's place. I drank little sips of water, trying to find my voice, trying to set aside what I'd done and how totally alien everything felt and focus back on the problem at hand.

"What the hell happened to Lia?" I finally made myself ask. "Do you think she saw the weasel and his pal and took off?"

"Maybe," Malloy said. "Maybe they already got her and were just waiting for us."

"Now what?"

"Now we need to get that 2257 information you mentioned for PDM Video," Malloy said. "See if we can get a drivers license on Lia."

"We can probably get it online at your place," I said.

Malloy nodded and ground out his cigarette in the ashtray.

"Do you have a breath mint or something?" I asked.

"Glove box," Malloy said.

I opened the glove box and dug through maps and napkins and things until I found a tin of Altoids. I popped it open and took one. Malloy turned onto Hollywood Way. As the candy dissolved on my tongue, the details of the events in the parking lot started to dissolve as well. Part of me felt it was important to hang on to them, to savor them in all their ugliness. But there was another part of me that was just as glad to let them go.

We drove in silence. Malloy turned onto his street and parked a few doors down from his place. I followed him along the sidewalk and over toward the door to the apartment complex.

"You know," I said. "This is gonna sound really weird, but I'm kinda hungry all of a sudden."

Inexplicably, Malloy froze. He did not reply. His body language turned simultaneously tense and fluid, like a cat that had just spotted a mouse. He slowly reached out and wrapped his fingers around my upper arm.

"What?" I asked.

"My wallet," he said. "I—"

Before he could finish the sentence, there was a sharp, sudden Fourth of July pop and a puff of plaster dust exploded from the wall about an asshair away from the left side of Malloy's head.

"Go!" he said, shoving me ahead of him so hard I nearly fell.

I have no idea how I managed to keep my feet under me and Malloy behind me as we barreled down the sidewalk with those firecracker pops going off all around us. That cliché you always hear about how everything goes into slow motion at times like this is kind of true, but also kind of not. The world around me was suddenly way too bright and sharp, everything crystal clear and intensely significant, but it also seemed like things were happening before my mind had time to sort them out. Like my brain was just a befuddled old grandma in my body's backseat, demanding to know where on earth we were going in such a hurry.

The next thing I knew my cheek was pressed against the battered door of an old Chevy Nova. Either the pops had stopped or I had gone totally deaf. All I could hear was ringing inside my ears. It seemed pretty comfortable and safe down there by the Nova and I felt like maybe I could use a little nap, but Malloy was dragging me again, impatient fingers digging into me and forcing me to leave the comfy Nova behind. He pushed me into his SUV through the driver's side door. I hit my chin on the steering wheel and nearly impaled myself on the gearshift but he was right behind me, shoving me aside, cranking the ignition and stomping on the gas before the door was even shut.

I thought I couldn't hear anymore but I was wrong. The sound of the rear windshield shattering was like the end of the world.

"Jesus!" Malloy said, wrenching the wheel from left to right and then reaching under the seat for my gun.

I guess you could call what happened next a car chase. It was probably pretty spectacular and exciting, with lots of near misses and bullets flying all around. I'm sure it would have been a blast to watch in a movie theater, but I'll tell you what, it's not nearly as much fun when you're jammed down into the place under the dashboard where your feet go, arms wrapped around your head and screaming at the top of your lungs, slamming from side to side like improperly stowed luggage and wishing you would die in a fiery wreck already, just to get it over with. I don't think I've ever been so scared in my life.

21.

But we didn't die in a fiery wreck. I felt the car slow, then stop and it took me a few seconds to get up the guts to uncover my face and risk a peek at our surroundings.

We were over by the L.A. River. There were no other cars in sight. Feeling beaten up all over again, I slowly unfolded myself from under the dashboard and crawled up into the passenger seat. My heart was still pounding so hard it felt like it was going to bust out like a baby alien and run off down the street.

I looked over at Malloy. He was gripping the wheel, breathing hard through his nose, his mouth a thin, tight line. He had a rapid tic in the bunched muscle at the hinge of his jaw and there was blood running down his neck, into the collar of his shirt. His right earlobe looked like a piece of red chewing gum.

There was a strange, indefinable charge in the air between us that felt almost sexual in its intensity but neither one of us did anything about it. We just sat like that for several minutes. Separate, not speaking. The motor idled. A sparrow perched in one of the diamonds on a nearby chain link fence. My heart slowly returned to a normal pace.

"I lost my wallet," Malloy said.

I frowned.

"What?"

"In the parking lot, back at the mall," he squinted at

the sparrow. “My pocket got torn while I was fighting with that guy you popped.” He tugged at the ragged flap in his trousers. “I guess my wallet must’ve fallen out.”

“Fuck,” I said softly. “Is that how they found your address?”

“Could have been a lot worse,” Malloy said, putting the car into gear. “Cops could have found it. My wallet next to a dead body. That would have been tough to explain.”

“Guess that means the bad guys found the body first, huh?” I said. “Think they took it?”

Malloy nodded and lit a cigarette.

“They don’t want cops in this any more than we do,” he said.

“Do we still need to get rid of the gun?” I asked.

“Couldn’t hurt,” Malloy said. “Don’t worry, I’ll get you another one.”

“Now what?” I asked.

I looked away. I felt bad for dragging Malloy into this mess but he didn’t seem all that sorry. He just smoked.

“For now, I say we hole up somewhere anonymous,” he said. “Somewhere with a DVD player.”

That’s how we wound up at the Palmview Court Motel.

The Palmview Court Motel got one thing right. The tiny office did feature a view of a dry, brown, rat-infested palm tree slowly dying from carbon monoxide poisoning. Most of the Palmview’s downwardly mobile clientele probably never bothered to look out their windows, since they were busy looking at the stained ceiling while turning tricks or at the insides of their eyelids while nodding out with needles in their arms. Not much in the charm department, but every room boasted its own DVD player, built into the bolted-down television.

The scrawny, hyperanimated tweaker behind the desk had a shoebox full of cheap porn compilation DVDs that a handwritten sign offered for two dollars a piece. When I asked about the DVD players, he rattled the box at me in a manner that I guess was meant to be enticing.

"The queer ones are mostly toward the bottom," the guy told me, weird blue eyes jittering around like they were trying to figure out a way to escape from their sockets. "Not that I got anything against queers. Takes all kinds, I guess. Anyway, if you return the DVD when you're done you can have one of your dollars back."

I kept on forgetting that I was supposed to be a boy. I couldn't help but wonder what Malloy thought about being constantly mistaken for some kind of gay Daddy. If it bothered him, he never let it show.

The DVDs in the box were the kind that promise SIX SIZZLING HOURS OF NONSTOP XXX ACTION but actually feature one so-so scene with a girl you've maybe heard of, along with endless hours of swimmy European crap from 1985. I didn't bother to dig for the gay ones. I was afraid to look too closely at the ones on top, in case there might be one of mine in there.

"No *Naughty Teens*," Malloy said, rifling through the box as I checked us in with cash and tried to avoid looking at the desk clerk's manic rictus of gray, rotten teeth. He bobbed and twitched nonstop behind the desk, like a puppet made out of beef jerky.

"Yeah well," the clerk replied. "If you don't see one you like, there's Le Sex Shoppe over on Van Nuys. Tell 'em Reno from the Palm sent you and you'll get a discount."

"Great," I said, feeling like I needed to wash my brain.

"Let's go," Malloy said.

Although I'd driven right past Le Sex Shoppe a billion times, I'd never actually been inside. I could get pretty much any dirty DVD I wanted for free since I used to write reviews for *AVN* and I got free toys from Doc Johnson because I used their stuff exclusively on our Web site. There'd never really been a reason for me to go to a place like Le Sex Shoppe. Until now.

A lot of people are surprised that these kinds of places are still booming, considering the fact that everything is available on the Internet. The truth is, there are still plenty of guys who share computers with their wives, guys who don't own computers, or guys who just prefer to pay cash for their smut. Places like that also feature video booths so guys with too much feminine supervision at home can rub out a quick one on their lunch hour.

"Here," Malloy said, indicating a row of similarly packaged DVDs in the amateur section. Sure enough, it was *Naughty Teens*.

Seeing them all side by side like that, I was suddenly hit with the sheer number of girls involved in this nasty business. There were twenty-one DVDs in a tidy row. Each DVD contained four or five scenes. Sure, there were a few repeats but still, that meant there had been nearly a hundred girls involved in this sex slave racket. It must cost a pretty penny to buy, house, feed and most importantly keep secret, such a large group of illegal foreign women. I couldn't imagine the meager sales of these DVDs alone provided enough income to make something like that profitable enough to be worth the risk.

I shared my thoughts with Malloy.

"It just seems odd to me that they don't bother to really shoot the hell out of each girl," I said. "A busy actress can shoot twenty-five scenes a month even without a gun to her head. These girls only do one or two scenes each. Why not get the maximum value out of their investments?"

"Lia said she'd been forced into prostitution, not just porno," Malloy said. He examined the DVD cover featuring "Kimberly" and Jesse Black. "My guess is these DVDs are just video catalogs thrown together to show off the available merchandise. The prostitution is probably where they make the real money."

"Jesus," I said softly.

"So," Malloy said. "Let's get that 2257 information."

Back at the Palmview, we settled into the dumpy room. It sucked, but at least no one was trying to shoot us.

The first thing I did was lock myself in the bathroom and unwind my binders. I was moist and sour from adrenaline and fear sweat and I felt like I would die if I didn't rinse off. There was no soap and the rusty, lukewarm water dribbled out of the showerhead like blood from the wrist of a reluctant suicide. Still, it was better than nothing.

When I got out of the shower, I dried myself gingerly with the bathroom's single rough, sort-of-white towel and then paused. There was a long skinny mirror on the back of the bathroom door, offering up a slightly warped view of my naked body from the knees up. Naked, it was impossible to pretend to be someone else.

I touched my scalp. My chin. My belly. The bruises

had faded to the point where you could almost pretend they were shadows. I took out the red lipstick I had stolen from Tabby and put some on. It sounds so weird now, but looking in the mirror at myself with those shiny red lips made me feel alive. Sexy. Real. They made me feel like me again. I decided in that moment that I would wear lipstick when I killed the bastard who set me up.

Malloy knocked softly on the door and I jumped, quickly wiping my lips on the back of my hand.

"Just a second," I said, putting the lipstick back in the pocket of my duffel bag that used to hold the gun.

I put on the clean t-shirt that wasn't the Lakers shirt. It was red and plain. Long, like a dress, like Lia's had been. I couldn't face the ace bandages again just yet so I gave my tits a break and let them be.

Malloy went silently into the bathroom after I came out. While he washed up, I called Roxette's cell again. It still went straight to voicemail. No one picked up at her house either. After that, I spent way too long battling the plastic wrap and all the security stickers holding the *Naughty Teens 17* DVD case shut. I was inches from flinging the damn thing out the window when Malloy came out of the bathroom, water beaded on his silver buzzcut and the crusted blood gone from beneath his ear. I handed the case over. He calmly slit the wrapping with a small pocketknife and extracted the disk.

He put in the DVD and I sat back on the bed. A red FBI warning came up, then the 2257 information.

This motion picture "NAUGHTY TEENS 17" was produced on July 12th 2006. The records required by U.S.C. Sec 2257 and 28 C.R.F. Part 25 for this motion picture and on any related materials to which this notice is affixed are kept at the offices of the manufacturer, PDM Productions, located at 13505 Cielo Street, Chatsworth CA 91311 by the custodian of records, B. Handerlan. All persons who appear in this video are over 18 years of age. For adult viewing only. Exercise your rights as an adult American citizen and enjoy all of the fine XXX videos available from PDM Productions.

There was no way to pause it, since there was no remote, but Malloy didn't seem to need to. He just wrote the address down. While he was writing, the menu came up. A large still of a brunette who wasn't Lia, looking more bewildered than sexy, filled the right side of the screen. The title was beneath her and a large square to the left framed a repeating trailer cobbled together from clips from the various scenes. One of the scenes was Lia with Jesse. Just seeing him made me feel physically sick. Malloy stood and hit stop. The screen went gray, but it didn't make me feel better.

"You okay?" he asked.

"I'll be better when he's dead," I replied.

22.

The PDM offices were just what I had been expecting. I'd never been there but I might as well have. The Valley was riddled with hundreds of places exactly like this. A warren of mildewy, over-airconditioned rooms up front and a huge hollow warehouse space in the back. A couple of indentured editors lurking lemur-eyed and unshaven in rooms lit only by images of grinding flesh. Mexican and Salvadoran ladies slipping slick printed covers into thousands of plastic DVD clamshells. Fulfillment girls and a forklift driver and some poor sod on QC, watching hour after mindless hour of smut in a never-ending hunt for digital glitches. A busy little beehive all working tirelessly, day in and day out, so that you can look at naughty movies in the comfort of your own home.

The 'B' in *B. Handerlan* turned out to stand for Barbara. She was blonde, plain and mushroom pale with the same expression of weary, put-upon exasperation worn by employees at the DMV. She acted as though the enormous effort involved in getting up out of her spavined chair and walking over to the file cabinet to find the records Malloy had requested was almost more than she could bear.

"We appreciate your assistance, Ms. Handerlan," Malloy told her.

"No problem," she said, making it clear that it was, in fact, a major problem. "What was the title again?"

"*Naughty Teens*," Malloy replied. "Seventeen."

"Right," the woman said.

While she searched noisily through the files, I let my eyes wander over her desk. She had a photo of two chubby boys in a frame that said "Mommy's Angels." A few more years and they'd be sneaking peeks at *Naughty Teens* themselves.

"Okay," she said. "*Naughty Teens 17*."

Malloy met her halfway and snatched the slim file from her hand.

"Thanks," he said, laying the file open on the desk and thumbing efficiently through the contents.

In seconds he had sorted through the model releases and found one for "Kimberly." The model release and attached drivers license scan said her name was not Kimberly or Lia, but Amanda Rose Temmens, age 19.

Malloy jotted down the number on the license and was about to snap the file shut when he paused. He frowned slightly and jotted something else down.

The woman had just made it back to the desk and was about to lower herself back down into her chair.

"Thank you, Ms. Handerlan," he said again. "One other thing."

Ms. Handerlan halted her descent toward the chair, scowling at the prospect of one more thing.

"What?" she asked.

"Do you have contact information for the person who actually shot this video?" Malloy asked.

"What?" she said again. "You mean the director?"

"Yes," Malloy said.

"Well…" she replied. "It should be on the release."

"I saw that," Malloy said. "But the address is a just a

PO box. Don't you have another address or maybe a phone number?"

"If we did," Ms. Handerlan said, "it would be on the release."

"Well," Malloy said. "What if something goes wrong with the film and you need to contact someone?"

She shrugged. "If it's not on the release, I can't help you. You'll have to talk to the owner."

"Okay," Malloy said. "Can I talk to the owner now?"

"He's not here," she said. "He's out of town."

Malloy seemed to realize that he had gotten all he was going to get out of her.

"Right," he said. "Thank you for your assistance."

The woman did not reply. Malloy shot me a look and gestured toward the door with his chin.

In the parking lot PDM shared with a chrome plating facility, a weight loss supplement company and a mysterious business whose sign read "J-Toc Fabrication," Malloy lit a cigarette and spoke low.

"Got a license on Jesse Black," he said.

Why hadn't I thought of that? Of course Jesse's release would have to be there too. Now that we had his real name and address, it would be a cinch to find him. The thought of it made me feel giddy—and a little nauseous.

"So now what?" I asked.

"I want to see what I can dig up on Amanda Rose Temmens," Malloy said. "I've got an old friend on the job who owes me, but you can't come. You'll need to stay at the motel."

I nodded, not really listening. I was still thinking about Jesse.

23.

I must have fallen asleep in the dim, musty cave of our room at the Palmview because it seemed like I'd only closed my eyes for a minute and Malloy was back. He brought Thai food, water and cigarettes.

"So?" I said. "Tell me."

"Eat first," Malloy said, offering me a takeout box and a plastic fork. "You haven't eaten all day."

I had been feeling kind of hungry right before the whole crazy shootout business and when I opened the little white box the fragrant, spicy steam brought it back in spades. I didn't even know what I was eating, but I wolfed it down.

Malloy ate too, slow and silent. His shoulders were hunched, eyes narrow and distant, looking at nothing while he chewed. I thought maybe there was something on his mind, something that wouldn't leave him alone, but it was so damn hard to tell with him.

"Well," I finally said. "Don't keep me in suspense."

"Okay," he said, setting down his paper box of noodles and wiping his lips with a crumpled napkin. "For starters, the license for Lia is phony. Amanda Rose Temmens died of Sudden Infant Death Syndrome at the age of five months."

"No shit," I said. "So does this mean we can blow the whistle on the guys who made the video?"

"We could," Malloy said. "But I'm guessing the boss of

this racket is way too sheltered to get popped. PDM would go down for distributing, maybe take a fall guy or two with 'em, but the D.A. would never get close to the boss."

"Okay," I said. "What else?"

"Well, my buddy who ran the license recognized the photo of Lia." Malloy said. "Apparently a Jane Doe came in after getting hit by a city bus on Vanowen and Vesper. The driver and several witnesses claim that she threw herself in front of the bus deliberately."

"He's sure it was Lia?" I asked, incredulous.

"The incident occurred half a block from your office less than five minutes after you say she went out your bathroom window. It's gotta be her. Her face was smashed up pretty bad, but they had a sketch done based on her bone structure and get this: They put the sketch out to see if anyone could ID her and a guy came forward. This guy, Jaime Martinez, claims he met her the night before she came to your office. Picked her up in a bar. She told him her name was Brittany."

I snorted and shook my head.

"Anyway," Malloy continued. "This Martinez guy took her back to his place. He said she acted real nervous and didn't have a car. When he left for work the next morning, he told her she could stay for a few days if she wanted to. She was gone when he came home."

"So," I said, trying to piece together what had happened, "she's with this Vukasin, the guy in the organization who she got to 'like her like a girlfriend,' when she steals the briefcase and bugs out. She can't get far with no car, so she ducks into a bar and picks up a guy with wheels. Gets him to take her to his place."

"When he goes to work the next day," Malloy said, "she starts snooping around, trying to come up with a plan. Maybe she finds the guy's porn stash and recognizes Zandora. Maybe she calls around and gets your name. There's a whole lot of maybes there, but somehow she finds her way to your office. Then those guys show up. Maybe someone she talked to tipped them off or maybe she took a taxi and they found her through the cab company. Either way she's fucked. She sees them coming, stashes the case and tries to make a run for it. When she realizes she can't get away..."

"Jesus," I said softly.

I tried to imagine how desperate she must have been to throw herself in front of a bus instead of allowing those bastards to get her back. How she must have been hoping with everything she had left in the last seconds of her life that her message had gotten through. That a childhood friend she hadn't seen for more than ten years would somehow find a way to help her kid sister. She could never have guessed how the events she set in motion would take down everyone around her.

I grabbed a bottle of water and twisted it open, taking a long drink.

"There's more," Malloy said, taking out a pack of cigarettes from an open carton. He lit one and put the pack in his pocket. "It's bad."

"Bad?" I asked, frowning. "Bad how?"

"I ran into Erlichman," he said. "He told me they confiscated your computer and sent it off to some company that searches around for hidden or deleted stuff. I don't really know exactly how it works but that's not the point.

The point is, they found some photos. Young girls, Angel. Real young."

"Son of a bitch," I whispered. I set the water bottle down hard, and stood, feeling like I'd taken a stiff kick to the chest.

My life was over. Period. Daring Angels and everything I'd worked for was dead as dog shit, as dead as I was supposed to be. Drugs, domestic violence, even murder, they were manageable offenses, but you didn't come back from a kiddie porn investigation. Not in this business. That bland-faced son of a bitch had done me good. He hadn't just tried to have me killed, he'd driven a stake through my livelihood and salted the earth for good measure. A cold choking fury was bubbling up again, stronger than ever. I wanted to break shit.

"They say you and Sam had a little kiddie porn thing going on the side," Malloy was saying. "They figure you decided to take Sam out of the loop. A business deal that went south."

I suddenly noticed how intently Malloy was looking at me. Squinting against the smoke from his cigarette, gauging my reaction.

"What?" I said, anger dangerously close to boiling over. "You don't seriously believe…"

"You were the one defending those teen girl movies," Malloy said. "You tell me."

I didn't even realize I was going to take a swing until I already had. Malloy was fast, but not quite fast enough and I grazed his stubbled chin with the tips of my knuckles. The cigarette flew out of his mouth and bounced off the carpet. I have no idea what I thought I was going to do, but I flung myself at him, throwing wild haymakers with everything I had behind them. He just grabbed me and spun me around so that my back was to his belly, holding me tight with my arms pinned to my sides. I flailed and kicked, furious and silent except for the harsh sound of my angry breath. I got him a couple of times pretty good on the shins and knees, but he was like a wall, patiently waiting out my tantrum. Eventually I got winded and started to feel stupid.

"You done?" Malloy asked.

"Fuck you," I spat.

"Look, Angel—"

"Fuck you for even thinking that about me," I said.

"I'm sorry," he said. "I had to know."

He let me go and I staggered away. I turned to face him and then sat down hard on the bed, elbows on my knees as I fought to catch my breath. Malloy sat back down in the chair and rubbed his left shin.

"Look," Malloy said. "I'm not a nice guy. I've done things I'm not proud of in my life but there's a line, you understand. Anything with kids, little girls like that, that's over the line. You want to kill a couple of guys who fucked you over, I'll help you, no questions asked. But I needed to know you wouldn't cross that line. It's important to me, Angel."

"Now you know," I said, looking up at him with narrowed eyes.

He held my gaze for a long time before he answered.

"Yeah," he finally said. "I guess I do."

Neither of us spoke. Outside, someone honked a horn and cursed in Spanish. I could smell thin, acrid smoke that got stronger and stronger and Malloy and I both realized what it was at the same moment.

"Shit," I said, as Malloy hurried across the room and stomped out the burning patch of carpet that had been ignited by the smoldering cigarette.

I coughed and waved my hand in front of my face while Malloy fumbled with the window, forcing it open.

"What, are you trying to burn the place down?" I asked.

"Probably not the first time someone set the carpet on fire in this joint," he replied. "Probably not the last either."

I laughed but it felt forced. The laugh died in my throat and I wrapped my arms around my body. I felt empty.

Malloy just looked out the window with his back to me. Nothing happened for several minutes, and then his cell phone rang.

"What is it, Didi?" he asked when he flipped open the phone.

His face went still and serious as he listened. Without another word, he handed the little phone to me.

"Didi?" I said.

"Angel," Didi said. Her voice was choppy and full of static. "I got a couple of dickless wonders with guns over here." There was a thump and clunk that sounded like she had dropped the phone. "Motherfucker!" she hollered. "Go ahead, hit me again you little shit. Hit me all you want, it ain't gonna make you grow a dick."

"Didi!" I shouted. "What the hell's going on?"

There was more static and then a very young-sounding male voice came on the line.

"Yo bitch, listen up," he said. "You get your ass over here ASA fucking P or your friend Didi is history."

I could hear Didi cursing in the background.

"Where are you?" I said. "Didi's house?"

"Just get here," the kid said and then the call had ended.

24.

The drive to Didi's house in Winnetka was tense and silent except for the rush of wind through the broken rear window. I was still reeling from the kiddie porn thing, but there was no room left in my head with all the fear for Didi and the aching guilt for dragging her down into this nightmare.

When Malloy pulled up in front of Didi's house, I could see a yellow Hummer parked in her driveway, looming over her little Saturn like a giant Tonka toy. The front door was open, just a crack.

Malloy gestured toward the gray Caprice parked across the street. The car was empty. "That's the same tail that was on Didi when she came by my place."

"The cops?" I said. "So where are they, inside? Maybe they already saved Didi and we can just..."

The flat crack of a gunshot echoed through Didi's house, followed immediately by another.

"Goddamn it!" Malloy said, tossing me a gun and swiftly drawing another. "Come on."

No time to think. No time to do anything but grab the heavy gun out of my lap and follow Malloy.

Inside Didi's cozy and familiar house, I felt a swift emotional sucker punch, a kind of bone-deep longing for Didi and my former life that was so powerful it made me nauseous. She had this big lacy teddy bear stuffed full of potpourri that sat on a shelf above the television. I always used to tell her that was the dumbest, ugliest thing ever, but she loved it. Now the familiar warm spicy peach smell of that potpourri bear was like a dead lover's perfume. I was glad it was so dark, because the walls around me were covered with framed photographs and every single one of those photos would have torn my heart out. In the dark they were just squares of glass.

I could hear a commotion toward the back of the house, in the playroom. Didi was like me but even more so: I never liked to actually sleep with anyone, but she took it a step further. She didn't allow her lovers into her bedroom at all. Didi and I have both been accused of having intimacy issues, but hey, when you show the world your private parts for a living, you need to find other ways of maintaining your privacy. Didi did it by having two totally separate rooms, one for sex and one for sleeping. The room for sex—the playroom, as she called it—was probably originally a rec room or family room of some sort. When she'd turned the little house into her own swinging bachelorette pad, she'd converted it into a groovy love lounge right out of one of her movies, circa 1979.

As I followed Malloy down the narrow hall, the sweet peachy scent was overwhelmed by something more raw and visceral. In the playroom, we entered a scene that would dig its way down into my brain and stay there for the rest of my life.

There were five men in the room. Three were dead and one was working on it.

The guy who was still hanging in there was some tattooed pretty boy who looked like he was in a band that would never get signed. He was in the far corner trying to get up on his hands and knees and not having much luck.

He had been shot in the throat and was making weird squeaky sounds that might have been funny but weren't.

The dead man to his left was well dressed in a Hollywood wannabe kind of way. He was tall and model-hunky and looked familiar. I was pretty sure he was in the business. Judging from the amount of extra weight inside the left leg of his tailored trousers, I'd say it was in front of the camera. He didn't seem like he belonged in this amateur hour clusterfuck.

The other two dead guys were obviously the plain-clothes cops from the Caprice. One was slumped over the padded love swing, chains clinking like the ghost of Jacob Marley as he swayed gently back and forth. His right shoe had fallen off, revealing a crumpled black sock with a small hole at the end. The hole wasn't big enough for his whole toe to poke out yet, but it probably would have been by the end of the shift, if he had stayed alive to keep on wearing it out. The other cop was on the floor about six feet from his partner, on his back. A leather wallet with a badge inside lay inches from his open hand.

The one unharmed guy in the room was crouching over the cop on the floor. He looked like he might be a bandmate of the dying pretty boy, also heavily inked, only not as pretty. Probably the drummer. He had what looked like a bloody white club held high over his head like a caveman. When he spotted us, an odd little grunt escaped his lips and he let the weapon drop.

When it hit the floor, the club jumped and started buzzing like an angry hornet, skittering across the carpet and dragging a long white tail behind it. I realized then that it was a vibrator. I don't know why, but I felt compelled to catch it and turn it off. It was something to concentrate on other than the nightmare around me. I tucked the gun into the back of my jeans and was about to grab the bloody vibrator by the cord and pull the plug out of the wall when Malloy shouted.

"Don't!"

I jumped, heart revving in my chest.

"Don't touch anything," Malloy said through his teeth.

I nodded and bit my lip. The vibrator continued its mindless racket. The guy crouching over the dead cop stared at Malloy with big blank eyes.

"Okay, genius," Malloy said, drawing a bead between the kid's wide eyes. "You want to tell me what the fuck happened here?"

"They…I…" was all the kid managed to say before he scrambled backwards off the dead cop and started puking down the front of his trendy faux vintage t-shirt.

"Lovely," Malloy said. "Looks like we missed this party."

"Where's Didi?" I asked. "Didi!"

The bathroom door on the other side of the huge circular bed was halfway open and there was blood on the doorframe.

"Didi!" I called again.

"Hurry up, Angel," Malloy said quietly. "There'll be probably be backup soon."

I ran to the bathroom and pushed the door the rest of the way open with the toe of my sneaker.

Didi was crouching by the toilet, holding one hand over the bowl. There were long streaks of crimson all down the front of her white, marabou-trimmed negligee. Her face was icy pale and sheened with sweat, her lips blue under smeared pink lipstick. The hand she held over the toilet had something horribly wrong with it, but

I couldn't stand to look too closely. The bowl was full of blood.

"It's about fucking time," Didi said. "Will you look at this?" She lifted her hand, or what was left of it. "That little prick shot me in my goddamn hand."

I ran to her and put my arms around her. She felt cold and slick, like some kind of sea animal.

"They said they were friends of Jesse's," she continued, leaning heavily against me. "Chickenshit son of a bitch was too much of a pussy to come himself, so he sends those bozos. I don't know the two ink monkeys, but the cute guy, that's Mitch Magnum's kid. Hung like his old man and just getting started in the business. Christ, what a fucking waste." She shook her head. "Then those cops showed up and the whole thing went to hell." She wiped her mouth on her forearm. "Look at my carpet. It's ruined."

"Come on, Didi," I said. "We gotta get you out of here."

"You cut off all your hair," she said, patting the back of my head with her good hand. "I don't know, honey. It kinda worked for Belladonna, but I don't think I like it on you. It makes you look…too dykey."

"I'll grow it back when all this is over, I promise," I said. "Now come on. Get up off your fat ass and let's get the hell out of here."

"I can't, Angel," Didi said, swallowing hard and pushing her sticky hair out of her eyes. "You go on."

"I won't leave you," I said, grabbing a silky fistful of her negligee. "Come on."

"Look, honey," Didi said, gently pushing my hand away. "I can't go anywhere like this. More cops are on the way, right? They'll take me to the hospital and get me fixed up. You can't go with me to the hospital, you'd get arrested."

"Bullshit," I said, feeling panic-stricken and desperate. "No."

"Go on," Didi said, pushing me away, but there was no strength in it. "I'll wait here. Maybe that sexy Detective Erlichman will show up and rescue me." She touched her sweaty hair. "How do I look?"

"You're a bloody mess, Didi!" I said, my throat clenched almost too tight to speak.

"Yeah well," Didi replied with a shaky smirk. "At least I got on something nice. Let this be a lesson to you, Angel. Always wear something nice, just in case. You never know when you'll get taken to the hospital and meet a well-hung doctor."

I looked down at my loose, unflattering t-shirt and jeans and was suddenly crying.

"Aw knock it off, willya?" Didi said. "I didn't mean what I said about your hair. It looks okay, really. I just need some time to get used to it, that's all. Now get out of here already. If you get yourself arrested on my account I'll kick your ass myself. One handed, even. Go!"

That's when I knew that she was dying. I could see it in her face, in her bright glassy eyes and tight smile. She had already lost way too much blood. There was no way she was going to make it.

I had always heard the word anguish, but I'd never really understood what it meant until that moment. Didi was the last connection I had to my old life. The last tie to who I'd been before all this. My house and my business were gone, but up until that moment, I could still count on Didi to back me up no matter what anybody said. I'd had no idea how much I needed that until I felt it slipping through my fingers.

"All right," I said, turning to leave with a cold vacuum under my sternum. I couldn't bring myself to say *goodbye* or *see you later* or anything like that so I didn't say anything more at all.

I paused by the door and looked back. Didi was resting her cheek against the toilet seat, her face turned away from me. I could hear sirens in the distance. What else could I do? I got the hell out of there.

25.

When we got back to the motel, there was no way I could sleep. I felt like I might never sleep again. When I refused to take the only bed, Malloy shrugged and took it himself without comment. He kicked off his shoes, took off his jacket, and put his gun and holster on the bedside table. He was asleep almost instantly, still dressed and on top of the covers. He lay straight as a board, on his back with his hands loosely clasped on his chest like a funeral parlor corpse ready to be viewed by the grieving family. He didn't snore. The only indication that he was still alive was the gentle rise and fall of his chest.

I just sat in that uncomfortable chair and didn't think. I waited for the sun to come up.

In the morning, the shit with Didi was on the news. She was already dead in my mind so when the inflatable blonde newslady announced that former porn star Diane Kellick, also known as Didi DeLite, had been shot to death in her Winnetka home, I felt nothing. They showed some old stills of Didi looking foxy back in the day with her blonde Farrah hair and sly smile. She would have been happy to be remembered that way. Handsome Detective Erlichman came on saying that they were currently unsure of the connection between the deceased guitarist of a local band called Smackdown and missing murder suspect Angel Dare. I laughed. I couldn't help it.

"What's so funny?" Malloy asked, coming out of the bathroom and rubbing the silver stubble on his chin.

"Nothing," I said. I shrugged. "Everything. I don't know."

"We've got that address from the drivers license," he said, putting on his jacket. "You ready to pay Jesse Black a visit?"

"I've been ready all night," I said. It sounded great. I hoped it was true.

"According to his model release," Malloy said, sipping 7-Eleven coffee as we waited to get on the 101 freeway, "Jesse Black is really Christopher Aaron Mezger. Born February 10, 1986. Currently residing at 1889 Draco Way. That's up in the West Hills near Bell Canyon Park. Nice."

I nodded, forcing myself to drink my own coffee, even though it tasted like hot varnish.

"For now, we just scope out the place," Malloy said. "Watch him and see where he goes. Who he's got with him. We need to figure out his routine so we can figure out how to get him alone."

"Right," I said. My head hurt. I knew it was going to be difficult not to blow the bastard out of his boots the second I set eyes on him again.

Jesse's house was beautiful and trashed. There were beer cans and discarded clothes and cigarette butts everywhere. Jesse's Ferrari was parked half on the driveway and half on the front lawn. There were several other expensive cars parked with varying degrees of competence all around the front of the house.

Malloy parked on the other side of the narrow street.

As we watched, a pair of girls, one blonde and one brunette, came out the door and wobbled down the walkway. They were built like greyhounds with implants and still dressed in expensive clubwear that was way too slutty for 9AM. You could see they had probably looked pretty good the night before, all made up and displayed under low-watt bar lighting. In the harsh light of day they looked rode hard and put away wet, raw red stubble burn around their mouths and raccoon smears of mascara all around their squinting eyes. Eventually the two of them found their way to a sporty little BMW two-seater and drove away.

Malloy and I waited. Several other young, attractive people came out of the house in various states of intoxication. It was nearly two hours before Jesse made an appearance.

He was wearing black-and-red track pants and a skin-tight tank top. His face looked pale, hung-over and puffy but he still looked beautiful.

Just seeing him made my heart twist savagely inside my chest. It felt almost like a toxic kind of crush. I wanted to kill him more than I've ever wanted anything in my life.

I might have done just what Malloy told me not to do, might have gotten out of the car and plugged the fucker right there in his driveway, but he had another guy with him. A black guy with a shaved head, an unattractive face and an astoundingly ripped and flawless body. The black guy was also wearing workout duds and it was no stretch to figure the two of them were going to the gym.

Malloy and I followed Jesse through his day and rapidly discovered that he was almost never alone. From the gym he and his buddy went to a pricey organic health food café called PURE where they met up with three gorgeous, interchangeable blondes. The buddy went off with two of the girls and Jesse took the third. They made a pretense of shopping along Ventura Boulevard and then she blew him a little in the Ferrari in the parking lot of the Bed Bath and Beyond. Jesse dropped her off back at the café and then headed over to a car repair place where he left the Ferrari and was picked up by another beautiful girl, a lush, full-figured Latina with a face like a young Sofia Loren. The caliber of tail that guy was getting was really unbelievable.

The new girl drove him out to the Vixen Video studio in Van Nuys. He dry-humped her for nearly half an hour before she let him out and drove away. He adjusted himself unselfconsciously and headed in to the studio. A few minutes later, I spotted hot Asian newcomer Heidi Ho lugging her gig bag across the parking lot. He wasn't inside long, just long enough to shoot one quick scene. When he came out, yet another beautiful girl picked him up, this one a tan, athletic fitness model type. She, too, made out with him for several minutes before dropping him back at the garage. Once he had his car back, he picked up a male friend at a coffee shop a few blocks away. The kid looked barely eighteen and extremely anxious. The two of them bought non-fat soy lattes to go and then headed over to a glass office tower on Ventura Boulevard in Tarzana.

"Holy shit," I said to Malloy as Jesse and his new friend headed into the lobby of the building. "You've got to be kidding."

"What?" Malloy asked, frowning.

"That's the office of Spotlight Escort," I said. "They hook up clients with well-known male porn stars. A lot of the guys do it, but I never would have guessed Jesse was gay for pay."

"No shit," Malloy said. "That's perfect."

"Perfect?" I asked. "How do you mean?"

"I mean that's how we'll get him."

26.

We left Jesse and his nervous friend and headed out to Panorama City. Our destination turned out to be a modest house that could have been any house on any working class street anywhere in Southern California.

Malloy made me wait in the car while he went up the walk and knocked on the door. A tiny, grandmotherly woman with bright orange hair and glasses on a beaded gold chain greeted him and ushered him inside, closing the door behind him. He was gone less than fifteen minutes.

"You want to tell me what that was all about?" I asked when he got back in the car.

"If we are going to rent Jesse," Malloy said. "We'll need a credit card. Here," He handed one of the cards to me. "I got one for you, too. Just in case."

"Is this a stolen credit card?" I asked, looking down at the card in my hand. The name on the card was Linda M. Kozlen. I just couldn't picture that old lady selling stolen credit cards.

"Yes," Malloy replied. "You got a better idea, let me know."

Malloy used his new card first to rent a Chrysler Sebring and then to book a room at the Woodland Hills Hilton. Then we made a visit to the Home Depot, for supplies.

It goes without saying that the Hilton was better than

the Palmview. I almost wished we could stay there. I took advantage of the clean bathroom to have a nice long hot shower. Malloy showered, too, and shaved and then called Spotlight from the hotel phone while I filled up my duffel bag with clean, fluffy towels and complimentary toiletries. It was amazing to hear Malloy's gruff voice go all soft and tentative, like a first time john.

"Um, yes, hello," he said. "I would like to book a date with…um…Jesse Black."

He arched an eyebrow at me when I came out of the bathroom.

"He doesn't?" Malloy said. "I see. Well, that's fine. I just…well, I just want…No, no fetishes." He paused. "No, kissing isn't important." Another pause "Look, I understand, but I really want Jesse."

I came over and sat down on the bed.

"Right," Malloy said looking down at the credit card. "Just the one hour. The name is Gerald Selbin. 'S' as in Snake, E-L-B-I-N." He shook out a cigarette. "That's correct." He sparked his lighter and dipped the cigarette into the flame. "Visa." He read off the number and expiration date. "Correct. Yes, I understand that the tip is not included. Hilton Woodland Hills. Room 403. Nine? Perfect. Thank you very much."

Malloy hung up and shook his head.

"What?" I said. I felt jittery and a little sick from anticipation.

"Jesse doesn't kiss, doesn't give head or handjobs, and won't let guys fuck him," Malloy said. "Strictly a top, they say."

"Yeah, well," I said, remembering his weight on me, his hands on my neck. "He's gonna bottom to me."

*

The wait until nine seemed endless. Malloy and I went over and over the details of the plan. It felt like waiting for my first date. I wanted everything to be perfect.

Jesse was twenty minutes late. By the time he finally showed up I was so high strung I nearly had a heart attack when he knocked on the door.

"Ready?" Malloy asked.

I nodded.

Malloy went to let Jesse in and I backed into the bathroom, closing the door down to a narrow crack I could peek through.

"You Gerald?" Jesse asked. I couldn't see him yet but just the sound of that lazy, cocksure California voice made my blood boil.

"That's right," Malloy said. "Please come in."

Jesse walked into my thin slice of a view. He was dressed in jeans and a black t-shirt that said STARFUCKER. His pretty blue eyes were distant, already deep in hustlerbot mode. This was going to be too easy.

"You look great," Malloy told him, taking out a hundred dollar bill and setting it on the bedside table. "You're even better in person than in your movies."

"Yeah," Jesse said, looking at the money and then off into space. "Thanks."

"Could you please..." Malloy said, flawless in the role of the anxious john, "your...I'd like very much to...see it."

"Right," Jesse replied, unzipping his fly.

While Jesse was concentrating on priming his pump for the job ahead, I quietly slipped out of the bathroom and pressed the snout of my pistol to the soft place where the back of his neck joined his skull.

"Get your fucking hands where I can see them," I said.

"Aw, shit," Jesse said, raising his hands up to shoulder level.

Malloy drew his gun and smiled.

"You remember Angel Dare," Malloy said. "Don't you?"

Jesse's eyes went wide. I pressed my gun harder against his neck.

"Am I still your favorite?" I asked him.

He didn't answer.

"Okay, listen up," Malloy said. "The three of us are gonna take a little walk."

"Can I...?" Jesse nodded down toward his exposed and rapidly shrinking livelihood. "Do you mind?"

"Go ahead," I said. "You won't be needing it anymore."

27.

We walked Jesse down the fire stairs and into the parking lot. I kept my arm around his waist as if he were my boyfriend, gun pressed into the small of his back under his t-shirt. Malloy was close behind.

There was nobody around as Malloy unlocked the new rental car and popped the trunk. Using a white plastic zip strip from Home Depot, Malloy swiftly bound Jesse's hands behind his back.

"Get in," I said, jabbing the muzzle of my gun into Jesse's kidney.

"You gotta be kidding," Jesse said.

"She's not." Malloy said.

"Come on now, Jesse," I said. "This is plush next to that damn Civic."

Malloy kicked Jesse in the back of one knee and his legs buckled. He fell face first into the trunk.

"Mother…" Jesse cried, but Malloy tossed Jesse's legs in after him and closed the trunk on *fucker*.

"Let's go," Malloy said.

Another long, silent drive, this one punctuated by rhythmic thumping and muffled curses from the trunk. I put on the radio and tuned to a classic rock station to drown Jesse out. Our destination was a place Malloy knew. A place out in the desert between Needles and nowhere. I didn't want to know why he knew about that place, but I was glad he did. It was perfect.

When we got there, we spent a couple of back-breaking hours digging deep into the stony, unwilling ground. The desert night was beautiful, cool blue and full of stars, a thousand stars serenely indifferent to what we were about to do.

Malloy muscled Jesse out of the trunk while I fetched a metal folding chair and a roll of duct tape from the back seat. When Jesse saw where he was and the freshly dug hole, he bolted, tripping and staggering and kicking up dust. Malloy chased him down easily and escorted him back, gun jammed up under his right ear. Malloy sat him down and I quickly duct taped him to the folding chair I had set up next to the hole.

"You're not gonna get away with this," Jesse spluttered, his face crimson and eyes wide.

"Start at the beginning," I said, showing him my gun again in case he'd forgotten about it.

"What?" he asked.

I slammed the butt of the gun into his left cheekbone. He yelped like a girl and almost went over backwards but Malloy caught the back of the chair with one hand. A thin trickle of blood ran down the side of Jesse's nose.

"Start with the briefcase full of money," I suggested.

"Okay, okay," Jesse said, looking down at the hole and then back up at me. "Fuck." He swallowed and licked his lips. "The money belongs to my uncle. It was payment for a new shipment of girls. Vukasin had the case and was supposed to bring it to the pick-up, only that little cunt got under his skin and managed to steal it while his pants were down."

"Vukasin?" I asked, remembering the unusual name from Lia's note.

"Vukasin, the Croatian guy who went to your office looking for Lia," Jesse said. "The short one. The one who isn't dead."

I nodded. So the weasel was Lia's "boyfriend."

"Okay," I said. "Tell me about this pick-up."

"Every six months or so, my uncle meets these guys at a warehouse near LAX. They give him six new girls and take six used up ones."

"Used up ones?" I said, exchanging a glance with Malloy who hung back, smoking. "What do you mean used up?"

"I mean the ones who don't look so good anymore," Jesse said. "The ones with HIV or Hep C, the ones that can't earn their keep anymore."

"Jesus," I said. "What happens to them after they get traded in?"

Jesse shrugged and smirked.

"They get to, like, go frolic and play in beautiful green fields," Jesse said. "Along with all the other little kitties and doggies and whores who can't work anymore."

I punched him in the face. I should have used the gun butt again because it hurt like hell, but I was pissed and didn't think it through. I just hit him.

"Fuck!" Jesse spat. "Fucking bitch. You want to know what they do? They sell them for cheap down in Mexico. Maybe they make tacos out of them. Or glue. How the fuck should I know what happens to a bunch of useless old skags?"

"Useless old skags?" I said, shaking out my hand and opening and closing my fingers. "What are they, nineteen? Younger than you, Jesse."

Jesse shrugged, sullen.

"Whatever," he said.

"How did you get involved in this?" I said.

"My uncle," Jesse said. "He's the boss. He owns the business with the girls. He owns all kinds of stuff. Real estate. Restaurants. He got me into doing movies, too. I did some on-camera work for him once and then I started getting calls from other directors who liked what I had and wanted to hire me. Next thing you know..." He shrugged, still full of himself, even with a gun to his head.

"And when did you start turning tricks to supplement your income?"

"Sex for money is sex for money," he said. "We're all whores on this train, Angel. You oughta know."

I refused to let him get a rise out of me. My knuckles hurt enough already.

"This uncle of yours," I said. "That's the guy with the bland face, right? The guy from the phony shoot who was asking all the questions."

"Yeah," Jesse said.

"And he's the boss, the one in charge of this whole sex slave racket? He's the one who framed me for Sam's murder and planted that kiddie porn on my computer, right?"

"Right," Jesse said.

"Tell me his name," I said.

Jesse squinted at me.

"I'm gonna find out eventually," I told him. I gestured toward the hole. "Better to just get it over with."

Jesse looked away like a petulant child. I bit my lower lip and kicked his chair over sideways. He tumbled face-first into the pit.

"Jesus fucking Christ!" he hollered, twisting his face to the side and spitting sand.

He was still taped to the chair, only now the chair was up on his back like some kind of weird turtle shell, its legs sticking straight out behind him. His ass was in the air, bound hands squirming and dark purple. His weight rested on his cheek and knees.

I picked up one of the shiny new shovels from the Home Depot and dumped a load of pebbles and sand on top of him.

"Alan!" Jesse said, sputtering and coughing. "His name is Alan Ridgeway! Alan Ridgeway!"

"He must be pretty pissed at you, huh?" I asked, squatting down beside the pit. "First you couldn't get it up to shoot me right like he told you to, and then you send those idiot friends of yours to get me instead of handling it yourself."

"Get me out of here," Jesse said, thrashing from side to side. "Fuck, get me out of here! I can't breathe!"

"Sucks, doesn't it?" I asked, letting him have another shovelful.

"Come on, Angel," he said. He tried to make his panicky voice softer. "I never meant to hurt you. It was my uncle. He made me do it. He planned the whole thing. He's the one you want, not me."

"Oh, don't worry," I said. "I'm gonna get him too."

Jesse kept on saying the kind of desperate shit men say when you've got them cornered. I didn't even bother to respond. I was thinking about what the hell I was going to do.

I had fantasized about this moment for so long. Dreaming of what I would do to Jesse once I got my hands on him. I had lulled myself to sleep at night with visions of choking him to death with my bare hands, burning him with cigarettes, making him feel violated and torn open like he made me feel. Now that I had my chance, I felt cold and strange.

I thought of how easy it would be to just keep on shoveling until I couldn't hear him anymore. It was a bad death, the kind of death a piece of shit like him deserved, but I found myself thinking of the way he had squeezed his eyes shut before he shot me. How he hadn't had the balls to look me in the eye. I didn't want to be like him. I wanted what happened between us in the end to be just as intimate as what he had done to me in that empty house in Bel Air. I wanted to look in his eyes when I did it.

I glanced over at Malloy and saw that he had gone back over to the car, still smoking and looking up at the stars. I guess he knew I needed to be alone for this.

I took a step closer to the edge of the pit and looked down at the gun Malloy had given me. It was a slightly older sibling of the Smith and Wesson I had used to plug the rhino. I tucked it into my jeans and slid down into the pit with Jesse.

He was crying when I landed beside him. It was hard to right the chair with him taped to it, especially in such a cramped space and with him outweighing me by fifty pounds at least. But I had a kind of hot, crazy focus that made me strong. When I got him upright he immediately started blubbering and begging me not to kill him. His face was muddy from snot and tears mixed with dirt. He looked so young, like a little kid who'd just gotten beat up in the schoolyard. I had to squint to make myself see the cocky bastard who'd had so much fun choking me until I passed out over and over again. I slid the gun out of my waistband and took his gritty, scraped up chin in my hand, looking into his beautiful blue eyes. He looked terrified, desperate. I didn't even know I was going to say anything until the words came out of my mouth. My line reading was way better than his had been.

"End of the line, bitch," I said.

Then I shot him.

28.

I buried Jesse. The soft plink of tiny rocks and sand hitting the metal chair seemed way too loud in the big desert night. I could have used some help, but I was glad Malloy hung back and left me to handle it alone. I needed the time to get my shit together.

It's not that I was freaked out or disturbed by what I had done. I don't exactly know how to describe what I was feeling as I buried the man who had raped me. Killing the rhino had been different. Impulsive. What I had done to Jesse, well, that was something else. In a way, it's like I was burying my old self in that pit. The person that I'd been before I'd looked into a man's eyes and shot him dead. The person that I was now, the delicate newborn killer that Jesse made me, needed the slow thoughtless shoveling like an insect still wet from metamorphosis needs time to dry its wings and figure out how to work its brand new form.

Because the killing wasn't over yet.

"Done?" Malloy asked when I finally came back to the car. He squinted at me, spit on his fingers and extinguished his cigarette. He put the butt into a small plastic bag filled with several others.

I nodded. It was chilly now that the physical labor was done but I barely felt it. As we quickly loaded the remaining equipment into the trunk, I saw a small, expensive cell phone and a scatter of change on the carpet inside the trunk. Probably fell out of Jesse's pocket while he was flailing around in there. I took the phone and put it into my duffel bag, figuring it might have some useful numbers. Malloy got into the car and motioned for me to get in, too.

"You got a little..." Malloy pointed to his chin and handed me a napkin from a Mexican restaurant.

I flipped down the visor and looked into the mirror. There were four perfectly round drops of blood like a small constellation on my face. One on my chin, one at the corner of my mouth, one just under my eye and one on my temple. As I wiped them away, I noticed that my bruises were almost completely healed. I still didn't look anything like I'd used to.

The radio had been on when Malloy killed the ignition and came back on too loudly when he started the car up again. The song was some sappy power ballad that had been popular when I first got into the business. I couldn't remember the name of the band and couldn't make myself care. Malloy reached to turn it off.

"Leave it," I said. I wanted to hear something that didn't matter.

Malloy nodded and put his hand back on the wheel. We didn't speak. Malloy drove back to the Palmview.

The sun was coming up as we pulled into the mostly empty lot of the Palmview. We both knew there wasn't any hope for sleep. I felt cold even though Malloy had given me his jacket again.

"You want coffee?" Malloy asked.

"Sure," I replied.

We went to a Starbucks down the block. I couldn't tolerate the clever, market-researched design of the place, so we took our expensive coffee back to the rental car and sat in the parking lot. Neither of us actually said *Now what*, but that's what we both were thinking.

"Roxette," I finally said. "I guess we need to figure out where the hell she went."

Malloy shrugged and sipped his coffee while I called her various numbers again. Again, no answer.

We wasted a couple of hours hitting all the places where Roxette could have been. Nothing. No one had seen or heard from her since last Friday before the meeting with Celestine.

"She could have taken the money and fucked off to South America by now," Malloy said.

I shook my head.

"She has money," I said. "Her folks are loaded and she's still pulling a huge day rate. She took the briefcase because she was curious, because she takes things. Not because she needed the money. Anyway it's locked with a combination. She probably hasn't even tried to open it."

"Ok, then where the hell is she?" Malloy asked. "Do you think she might have fallen off the wagon?"

"Maybe," I said.

"Meth was her drug of choice, right?" Malloy asked.

"Yeah," I replied.

"So if she wanted to get back into it, who would she call? Who would hook her up?"

I knew exactly who would hook her up, but just thinking his name made me queasy.

If you spend any amount of time working in the porn industry, you quickly get numb to drug casualties, just like you get numb to prolapsed rectums on set and guys sticking needles in their johnsons and all the other workaday atrocities of the modern smut racket. But I have to admit the sordid downward spiral of Thick Vic Ventura got under my skin. Not just because we had been lovers off camera, but because he had been so smart and funny. So real. So much like me.

Vic was from the South Side of Chicago, like me. Italian like me. His real name was Joey Pagliuca. He'd gone to high school with my brothers at St. Laurence and dated a girl two grades ahead of me at Queen of Peace. He'd left for Hollywood when I was just a freshman. He'd looked like a rock star, with his tattoos and long black hair—not exactly handsome, but charismatic. He had come to L.A. with ambitions to be a stand-up comedian. He was irreverent, sharp and wickedly sarcastic, but his comedy act had never caught on. In the end, it wasn't his dirty jokes but his astounding endowment that made him famous and gave him the nickname Thick Vic.

Like a lot of guys blessed (or cursed) with freakishly enormous dicks, he sometimes had trouble getting it up. It never really got all the way hard and he always joked that if it ever did, he would pass out from lack of blood to his brain. Still, with a good tight grip on the base, he was able to squeeze enough blood into the top nine inches to get the job done.

That was on camera. Off camera it didn't much matter to me. So many guys think they won't be able to cut the mustard with me because they aren't packing thirteen concrete inches. The truth is, the biggest, hardest dick in the world is useless if you don't know how to eat pussy; and Vic not only knew how to eat pussy but genuinely enjoyed it. He was one of the best lovers I've ever had.

But unsurprisingly, after a few years in the industry, the rock star lifestyle and hard partying took its toll on him. It got tougher and tougher for him to perform and he started getting a reputation for unreliable wood. A reputation like that is a death sentence for male talent.

Anything approaching real "dating" in the porn industry is challenging at best. When one partner is on the way up and the other on the way down, emotional disaster is pretty much a forgone conclusion. *A Porn Star Is Born*. When Vic stopped getting calls, he started getting clingy and jealous. He threw macho Italian temper tantrums in public places and we started having more screaming fights than screaming orgasms. His drinking and drug use got more and more out of control. It would have only been a matter of time before he pulled a Cal Jammer and blew his brains out in my driveway, so I put the relationship out of its misery. I don't think I personally sent him over the edge, since he was already well on his way before I kicked him to the curb, but I'm sure he'd tell you different. The last I heard of Thick Vic, he had failed his third attempt at rehab and was making ends meet by dealing methamphetamines to girls in the business.

When I'd first met Roxette, she had laughingly admitted that she used to party with Thick Vic before her drug-induced heart attack. She told me that he was still hung up on me after all these years and when the meth psychosis got really bad, he often thought she was Angel Dare.

I didn't tell any of this to Malloy. I just told him I thought I knew a guy who might know where Roxette had gone to ground.

Finding Thick Vic wasn't hard. A couple three phone calls and we discovered he was currently mooching off has-been plastic surgery casualty Taylor Simone.

Taylor was big around the same time that I was. Pretty in that standard blonde California way that everybody was back then. We did a few scenes together but all I remember about her was the fact that she ate pussy like a dog playing tug-of-war and left me raw for days. She lived out in Valley Village, near the freeway. Her sad little house was a disaster of strewn lingerie and chihuahuas and vodka bottles. She came to the door dressed only in little kid's Batman boxer shorts and a tan. She looked worse than I could have imagined.

I was amazed that someone so thin was able to stand up without assistance, let alone counterbalance the fifty pound pair of silicone beach balls shrink-wrapped to the front of her box-kite ribcage. Under her frazzled blonde weave, her face was a cheap doll's face, flash frozen and nerve-dead from too much surgery. Her nails were crooked pink sloth-hooks and her bony, nervous hands made clutching, Nosferatu shadows across her concave belly. She had drenched herself in cloying, sugary perfume that smelled like the kind of cheap vanilla frosting that comes in a can.

I have never understood this new trend where girls who don't eat anything but lettuce and ice cubes want to smell like cupcakes. On Taylor, the childish scent was made far worse by its inability to mask the toxic booze-breath and the underlying corruption of her slowly dying flesh. She made no attempt to cover her freakshow tits as she stood in the doorway glaring at us.

"Are you here to get that girl?" she asked.

Malloy and I exchanged puzzled looks.

"We're looking for Vic," Malloy said.

"He went to find someone to help get that fucking psycho bitch out of my bathroom," Taylor said. She gestured down a dim, cluttered hallway to her right. "If he doesn't get back soon, I'm gonna call the cops and let them know they can take him too for all I care. You see if I don't."

"Do you have any idea who you're fucking with?" a hoarse voice shouted. *"Do you? You don't know who I am!"*

It was Roxette.

Suddenly, Taylor was crying. Her frozen face struggled to crumple into something like a human expression but all she could really do was open and close her bloated lips, like a dying fish.

"I told him not to bring girls here anymore," Taylor said, leaning heavily into the doorframe. "What he does on his own time is his business, but this is my house. It's *my* house."

"That's terrible," Malloy said, taking her by the shoulder and gently moving her out of the doorway so we could enter. "You let him live under your roof, the least he could do is treat you with some respect."

"That's exactly what I mean," Taylor said, looking up at Malloy. "I'm not the jealous type. I don't want to run his life, I just want respect in my own house. Is that so much to ask?"

"Of course not," Malloy said, motioning for me to shut the door. When it was closed, he caught my eye over the top of her head, gestured toward the bathroom door with his chin.

I left Malloy with Taylor and headed down the hallway toward the bathroom where I had heard Roxette's voice.

"Roxette," I said, knocking tentatively on the door.

"I know what you're trying to do," Roxette replied. "I'm not stupid."

"I don't think you're stupid, Roxette," I said. "Why don't you open the door and we can talk about it?"

"You think I don't know about the transmitter?" she whispered. "I know all about the transmitter."

I shook my head. This was going to be really bad. I took a deep breath and took a gamble.

"Roxette," I said again. "Roxette, it's Angel."

"Angel?" Roxette's voice sounded suddenly anxious and childlike.

"Can I come in?" I asked.

"How do I know it's really you?" Roxette asked, voice suddenly closer as if she had just pressed up against the other side of the door. "What shoes was I wearing on the day we met?"

I rolled my eyes. That was nearly a year ago. I couldn't even remember what shoes *I* had been wearing that day. I tried to focus on recalling Roxette's feet. It had been the middle of a hot San Fernando summer and I seemed to remember her painted toenails so the shoes must have been open toed. Sandals of some kind, but that was the best I could do. I was drawing a blank.

"I'm sorry," I said. "I can't remember."

A jagged sob sounded behind the door.

"I can't remember either," Roxette said, bawling like her heart had just been broken. I heard a rhythmic thumping and was pretty sure she was hitting her head against the door.

"Please, Roxette," I said. "Just open the door a little ways. I won't try to come in if you don't want me to, okay?"

The thumping stopped.

"Okay," she said suddenly, like it had never been any big deal.

I heard the lock disengage and then a sweaty slice of Roxette's face appeared in a narrow crack, a single pinhole-pupiled eye staring out at me like the eye of a trapped animal.

"Oh my god," Roxette said. "They cut your hair!"

A hot, skinny hand reached out and pulled me into the bathroom.

Taylor's bathroom looked like it had been designed for a life-sized Barbie. Pink on pink with pink trim, pink carpet, even a pink toilet. The added splashes of irregular crimson clashed violently with the girly bubblegum color scheme.

Roxette was naked and icy pale. It was nothing most of America hadn't seen before, but there was a new addition. She had a hole in the top of her right thigh. In her hand she clutched a pink toothbrush, its bristles clogged with blood. There were bandages all over the floor and I could see a flat, pancaked bullet in the bottom of the pink toilet. It wasn't a stretch to figure she had dug that bullet out of her leg with the toothbrush. I was horrified when she turned away from me and went back to work on the hole with the bloody bristles.

"I'm pretty sure I got most of the transmitter out," she told me, not looking up from her task. "But they make them so they can rebuild themselves if even one tiny piece is left so you just can't be too careful."

"Who did this to you?" I asked. "Who shot you, Roxette?"

"It was those guys my dad sent to spy on me," she told me. "They have cameras in their eyes that transmit back to his office by satellite. You think that's just in the movies, but you're wrong. My dad owns the company that invented the technology for eye cameras. If you don't believe me, just watch the Discovery Channel. See, as soon as my dad found out I had the briefcase, he told them to shoot me with a transmitter bullet so they could track me. They thought I didn't know about the transmitter but ha ha because I showed them, didn't I? I got away and showed them."

"You sure did," I said, trying not to look at what she was doing to her leg. "What happened to the briefcase, Roxette?"

She gestured at a sopping pile of towels in the bathtub. "I covered it with wet towels to block the signal. Now I need to get to Vancouver before 3AM tonight or else..."

She looked up, suddenly confused.

"Who are you?" she asked.

"It's me, Angel," I said.

"How do I know it's really you?" she asked.

I was losing ground.

"They poisoned my cat," she told me. "I found his head in my purse."

She went back to her scrubbing.

I figured Vukasin must have been the one who shot her. Either him or one of Ridgeway's other errand boys. Whoever stole the security tape from my building had probably just methodically gone down the list of every single recognizable person who had visited my office that day. Roxette is pretty recognizable. She would have been easy to find. I couldn't imagine how she'd managed to get away from whoever shot her without losing the briefcase, but whatever had happened it had clearly sent her over the edge. Instead of going to the cops, she'd gone to Thick Vic Ventura.

I struggled to come up with some way to get her to give me the briefcase, some clever ruse that would dovetail into her ever-shifting psychosis, but I just couldn't think of a thing. In the end, I didn't have to. She made me take it.

"Oh my God!" she said suddenly, whirling around and gripping my arm way harder than you'd think a skinny little thing like her could. "God fucking god, I need you to do me this really huge favor."

"Okay," I said warily, trying to extract myself from her grip and failing.

"You need to take the transmitters to the Channel 7 news."

"Sure," I said, trying to keep a neutral expression as she pressed her hot face closer to mine. Her eyes were both vacant and terrifying.

"You have to swear on your own grave," she said. "Swear or you'll die seven times."

"I swear on my own grave," I said, trying not to cringe away.

"Okay," she said, suddenly breaking away and circling in a tight zoo animal orbit. "Okay okay okay. We'll need a towel."

I got one of the sopping wet towels out of the bathtub while she fished the bullet out of the toilet. I held the towel out to her and she deposited the flattened bullet on the towel's sagging center. Then she wrapped the bullet up in another towel and handed the bundle back to me.

"Take this too," she said, scooping up the briefcase and pressing it into my arms. "And the cat head."

She picked up a pink net bath poof and spoke gently to it before setting it carefully on top of my dripping burden.

"Hurry," Roxette said. "You have to make the seven o'clock news on Channel 7. Remember you swore on your own grave, Charlie."

I had no idea who Charlie was, but at that point all I cared about was getting the hell out of there.

"I swear," I said.

She hustled me out the door and swiftly locked it behind me. As soon as I reached the end of the hallway, I ditched the wet towels, the bullet and the bath poof and set the briefcase down on the carpet. It took me a second of staring at the little brass line-up of three numbered wheels to remember the combination I had seen Lia use in my office that day. 666. The number of the beast.

Maybe Roxette's meth-induced madness was catching or maybe it was just my own sleep-deprived state of mind, but as I popped open the latches I had a sudden irrational fear that the case would contain not money but something awful. It took everything I had to make my hands push open that case.

It was full of money, just like Ridgeway had said. There was no time to count, but it looked like a lot. Brick upon brick of banded hundreds, along with Lia's original handwritten note. I closed the case. I'd count the money later.

When I got back into the living room, I found Malloy grimly battling to maintain his virtue and keep Taylor's fingers out of his fly. A fat white chihuahua was furiously humping his leg.

"Come on, baby," Taylor was saying. "Don't be shy."

"Christ," Malloy said. "What took you so long?"

He extricated himself from Taylor's boozy affections and looked down at the briefcase, eyes widening. As he pried himself loose, Taylor burst into braying sobs.

"Let's get the hell out of here," I said. "Before—"

Of course, that was the moment Thick Vic picked to show back up with the cavalry that was supposed to help get Roxette out of the bathroom.

His assistants were a couple of aging bikers, a hamburger and hotdog pair with matching leather vests and matching scars. The burger was short and barrel-shaped with more white hair on his chinless face than on his large shiny head. The hotdog was tall and scrawny with his long black hair bound into two braids like that Indian who used to cry about pollution on TV. Turned out that guy wasn't really Native American after all. I didn't think this guy was either.

Seeing Vic again after nearly ten years probably would have been a lot tougher if the girl who used to care about him hadn't been buried out in the desert along with Jesse Black. Standing there in Taylor Simone's living room holding a briefcase full of stolen cash, I just sized Vic up along with his two buddies and decided they posed no threat.

Vic's long dark hair was mostly gone and what was left had been scraped back into a frizzy little ponytail. His fragile, skeletal physique made the desk clerk at the

Palmview look like Arnold Schwarzenegger and his face and arms were pocked with scars and scabs from needles and endless picking at imaginary crank bugs. If you slugged him, he would probably fall into a heap of dust on the piss-stained carpet.

"Get your shit and get the fuck out," Taylor screeched suddenly, reaching for Malloy. "I got a new boyfriend now who respects me, you junkie piece of shit."

"Jesus," Malloy said, stepping back out of her desperate grasp.

"You lying fucking whore!" Vic hollered. "You told me you were still sore from that last surgery and now you're banging some other guy behind my back?"

"Maybe if you could make that big dead thing between your legs do something other than lay there like a fucking roadkill snake," Taylor said, staggering to her feet, "I wouldn't have to go for other guys!"

"I got no problem getting it up for Roxette," Vic said.

Taylor let out a shriek and launched herself at Vic. The two of them tumbled awkwardly to the floor, sending platform heels and panties flying in their wake. The two bikers looked at me and Malloy and shrugged. The hotdog lit a cigarette and the burger wandered into the kitchen. Roxette was still howling in the bathroom. Malloy got a light from the hotdog and motioned toward the door. Vic and Taylor crashed into a spindly wire CD tower that was sturdier than either of them, knocking it over and scattering disks and splintered jewel cases across the carpet. No one seemed to notice the briefcase. No one tried to stop us when we left.

*

Nowhere to go but back to the Palmview. Malloy left to return the rental car and get food and cigarettes. I sat numbly on the bed with the duffel bag containing my meager worldly possessions and the briefcase containing what counted out to exactly one hundred and eighty thousand dollars.

I still felt raw and strange from the bad business with Jesse and beneath that was the dull, constant ache of grief over Didi and Sam. Over my house and my business and everything that used to matter. There didn't seem to be any kind of order or logic to this madness. Crazy, random things just kept on happening, dragging me along behind them on an unbreakable choke chain. I really wanted to be some kind of badass avenging angel, and standing over Jesse's grave I'd almost felt like I could be, but now I felt scattered and unfocused. I couldn't find my way back up into the driver's seat.

This game was far from over and wouldn't be over until Ridgeway was dead. Killing Jesse was a start, but the truth was, Jesse was just a tool. It was Ridgeway who was calling all the shots and I couldn't let myself disintegrate before I got to him. In the meantime, I needed to do something I could be sure of. Something to take control.

So I did two things. First I took the money out of the briefcase and packed it into my duffel bag, refilling the case with hand towels and toiletries from the Hilton until the weight felt right. Then I pulled on the stiletto-heeled designer boots.

When Malloy returned, I stood by the bed, facing the door. Hip cocked, smiling. I was naked except for the boots. My lips were slick with the cheap red lipstick. Even with the short hair, I knew I looked damn good. I looked like a woman.

"Lalo," I said. "Come here."

Malloy cautiously set his grocery bag down on the little table, pushing the door shut behind him.

"Angel..." he said, but I didn't let him finish.

I could feel him fighting himself, trying to hold back and stay cool but I knew it couldn't last. After all, I am a professional. I broke through his resistance as easily as he had taken down that thug in Vegas.

The raw lust that sprang free from behind that wall of stoic resistance was intoxicating. I needed it like other people need air and I filled myself up with it, gorged myself on it as he lifted me off my feet, holding me breathless against him and then tossing me down onto the rickety bed. He came down after me, heavy and eager, big hands all over me just like I wanted. But when I reached down to unzip his trousers, the wall was back as he suddenly dodged me, rolling away to one side.

"Angel," he said again. "I..."

I tried to kiss him again, but he wouldn't let me. His face was flushed pink, his eyes narrow.

"Look, Angel," he said.

"What?" I asked.

I had a sudden chilly fear that he would turn out to be the kind of guy who can't get past the porn star thing. The kind of guy who's turned off by the sheer number of priors. But my instinct told me he wasn't turned off in the slightest. His body was practically vibrating with leashed desire. I couldn't imagine what was holding him back until he spoke.

"I..." he said, eyes cutting away from mine. "I'm not...built like those guys in your movies."

It took everything I had not to burst out laughing. That's what this was about? Macho tough guy Malloy was worried that his dick was too small to satisfy Angel Dare? I can't tell you the number of times I'd heard those exact words or variations on that theme, but I never in a million years expected to hear it from Malloy.

I reached down and put my hand on what he had. He was no Thick Vic, but like most guys he was selling himself short.

"It doesn't matter," I told him.

Then I proved it.

After, we lay side by side, close but not touching. I can't say that I felt like my old self. I didn't think I'd ever really feel like that again, but I felt like a stronger and more focused version of whoever this new person was. Malloy got up and padded over to the table to get out another carton of cigarettes. He wasn't some kind of Hollywood muscle boy, but he looked good naked.

"Maybe we should get the hell out of Dodge," Malloy said, back half-turned as he tore open the carton.

"What do you mean?" I asked, leaning up on one elbow.

"I mean just say fuck it," Malloy replied, shaking a cigarette loose from a new pack. "Go to Belize or something. I don't know."

"You want to run away with me, Lalo?" I asked, smiling just a little.

He shrugged and lit up the cigarette then came back

over to the bed, lying back and throwing one thick arm up behind his head.

"Would that be so bad?" he asked.

Would it? He was a good lover. Earnest, quietly intense and focused on giving me pleasure. He was also apparently not into the kind of over-the-top theatrics that seem to be a given these days when everyone has gotten their idea of good sex from porn. Guys get with a porn star and they think that kind of shit is what we really want every day. Here's a tip for you. We do the things we do in porn because they look good, not because they feel good. Anyone who's ever done an airtight reverse cowgirl will tell you that, and I'm not just talking about the girls either. Luckily I didn't have to explain any of this to Malloy. And more importantly, he didn't try to snuggle. He just smoked and gave me space.

It's not like I had anything left in L.A. either. Didi was dead. Daring Angels was dead. Angel Dare was dead, or the next best thing. Up until that minute, I hadn't given any thought to anything but revenge. Could there really be some new kind of life for me now? Some way to start over?

Maybe, I thought, I really should quit while I was ahead. I had one hundred and eighty grand of Ridgeway's cash as payback for what he put me through. Couldn't I call it even and disappear? Me and Malloy. Why not?

I knew perfectly well why not. Because as long as that bastard Ridgeway was alive, I would never be at peace. I couldn't let it go. Maybe I should have, but I couldn't.

"No," I said. "I can't go anywhere until that son of a bitch gets what's coming to him. I just can't, Lalo."

"Getting to Ridgeway isn't gonna be easy," Malloy said. "It may be impossible. It's not unlikely that he'll get to you first. Guys like him almost never get what's coming to them."

"I understand," I said. "But I have to keep trying. It's all I've got left."

Malloy nodded, smoked and said nothing. After a minute or two passed, he spoke.

"After my wife left me and took Paloma back to Santa Fe," he said. "I didn't date anyone for a long time. I mean sure, I fucked around, but I never let any women get to me. I was drinking back then and didn't give much of a damn about anything. Then I met someone. She was a pro, you know? A call girl, but she never took a dime from me. Her name was Carla. She was from El Salvador. Long legs. Beautiful. Guys would line up to be with her."

I didn't say anything.

"One of her customers killed her," he said. "Strangled her." He took the cigarette out of his mouth and touched his lips with his thumb. "We knew who did it but we couldn't make it stick. He walked."

I turned to look at him. He didn't look back at me. His gaze stayed fixed on the water-stained ceiling.

"The guy was this low-rent Hollywood sleazebag," Malloy continued. "But he was connected. He had good lawyers. Carla, she was just another dead call girl. She didn't matter, and so the guy walked."

He took a long drag on the cigarette.

"It took three years, but I got to the guy," Malloy said. "I took him out to the desert and made him sorry for what he did. Then I killed him."

Malloy's cigarette was burned down almost to the filter. He crushed it out in the cheap glass ashtray on the built-in nightstand.

"For those three years," he said. "I couldn't think about anything else. Planning to kill that guy ate up every second I was awake and all my dreams too. I had nothing else. I made stupid mistakes on the job. Nearly got myself killed. All because I couldn't think about anything but how I was going to get that guy. For Carla." He got out another cigarette and lit up. "The drinking got out of hand. I lost my badge. I deserved it, too. I was a fuck-up and I knew it, but I just couldn't stop. It was like being in love, you know. Only hate."

Man, did I know. That was exactly how I had felt about Jesse. I still felt that way about Ridgeway. If you would have told me how much I had in common with someone like Malloy two weeks before, I would have laughed. Now I felt like he was the one person on earth who understood what I was going through.

"When it was over," he continued, "when I'd watched that fucker take his last breath, I realized I didn't feel any different. I didn't miss her any less. I'd devoted my whole life to getting that guy and once it was done, I didn't know what to do with myself. I thought it would be this great victory but it wasn't." He turned to me. "I guess I'm just trying to say that revenge isn't all it's cracked up to be. That's all."

I sat up and tried to run my fingers through hair that wasn't there anymore. I knew he was right. I wanted to run away with him and find some new kind of person to be. To start over someplace where no one had ever heard of Angel Dare. I wanted that, but I knew I wasn't going to have it.

"I know you're right," I said. "I do. But I can't walk away until this is done. Maybe after…"

I trailed off, unable to finish. I don't think either of us really believed in after anymore.

Malloy looked away. He seemed to be wrestling with something big, trying to find words that just wouldn't come. In the end he just said, "Okay, Angel. If that's how you want it."

"I'll show you how I want it," I said.

It was a cheap ploy, nothing but fleshy distraction from all the things I didn't want to think about. Our hearts weren't really in it. But we went through the motions anyway, just to have something to do. When it was done, I could feel exhaustion catching up with me. I tried to count the hours since I had last slept, but fell asleep counting.

I slept for what felt like forever and then came awake suddenly to the sound of pounding on the door. I was groggy and stupid but adrenaline quickly got my body clothed and upright. Standing, I realized two things at once. Malloy was gone. So was the briefcase.

29.

I didn't have time to feel angry or betrayed because I was too busy feeling like I was living my last ten seconds on this earth. I grabbed my duffel off the carpet and bolted into the bathroom. The Mickey Mouse lock on the bathroom door was a joke, but it might buy me an extra ten seconds, which at that point felt like doubling my lifespan. Standing in that shitty little bathroom, I was determined not to die there. I looked up at the tiny window and thought of Lia. I wondered if I would have the balls to throw myself in front of a bus if it came down to that.

Whoever had been banging on the door was in now, and had started on the bathroom door. I had no idea if they were cops or crooks and didn't care to find out which. The bathroom window didn't want to open more than a few inches, so I yanked down the shower curtain and wrapped it around my fist. It took more than one punch but eventually the thick, grimy glass gave way. I tossed the duffel ahead of me, hoping with irrational desperation that my blue coffee cup wouldn't break. I didn't even feel the jagged glass clawing at me as I squeezed through the window frame.

I had completely forgotten that I fell asleep in the spike-heeled boots until I hit the concrete. One slender, six-hundred-dollar heel snapped off and I felt my ankle twist, sending a jolt of pain up my leg. I looked both ways down the trash-strewn alley. I knew I couldn't run on a broken heel, so before I could give it too much thought, I opened a big rusty dumpster, tossed my duffel in and dove in after it, pulling the lid down tight.

Visceral memories of my trash bag dress sank nails into my stomach as I pulled rancid, leaking garbage bags over myself, tucking my head down and silently praying for the first time since the first grade.

I heard men's voices and running footsteps on the concrete. Then nothing.

My ankle throbbed. My head hurt. The smell was unbearable even with my t-shirt pulled up over my nose. As the adrenaline slowly ebbed away, I struggled to wrap my brain around what Malloy had done.

I had told myself again and again not to trust him, not to be a dependent little damsel in distress, but it had been way too easy to let him drive. Now that he had fucked off and left me, I felt this invisible wound that drained my resolve and replaced it with dull, hopeless anger. On the surface, my feminine ego was bruised, knowing that my bedroom blackbelt hadn't been enough to make him stay. But underneath was so much more. I'd thought he was my friend. I'd thought that meant something. I should have known better.

I waited in the dumpster way longer than I really had to, just to be sure, and even then I could feel myself cringing as I eased the lid open, ready for a bullet.

There was no one in the alley. At least that's what I thought at first. When I set my uneven boots on the ground, I noticed that a shape I had initially mistaken for a pile of trash was really a man. When I saw a glint of silver hair beneath the dirty crimson, I felt my stomach twist. I knew it was Malloy.

I wanted to go the other way and never look back, but I had to be sure. I limped over to where he lay, face down in an oily puddle. I was grateful for his position because there was a small neat hole in the back of his head. I'm no ballistics expert, but even I know that the little hole is where the bullet went in. There would be a much bigger, much uglier hole on the other side, where the bullet came out. The other side would be his face. I didn't need to see that.

A few feet away from him was the open briefcase. The towels and toiletries that I had used to fill it up while Malloy was getting cigarettes were scattered down the alley as if the briefcase had been opened, thrown down and kicked over to the wall. I didn't know why I had put the money in my duffel bag the night before. Maybe I'd had some sense of what might happen. I wondered if Malloy had decided to skate with the money after I refused to blow town with him, or if he had been planning on taking the money from day one and only asked me to come with him because he got soft after he got a taste of me. I wondered if he'd seen the towels before he died.

I wanted to feel sad, to mourn for this man who had rescued me and fucked me and betrayed me, but all I felt was a giddy, weightless sense of purpose. I felt streamlined, stripped down to fighting weight. I had absolutely nothing left. Nothing standing between me and Alan Ridgeway.

I retrieved Malloy's keys from his pocket and crept around to the front of the Palmview, trying to grow eyes in the back of my head. No cops. No crooks. Nobody except a single scraggly tweaker pacing barefoot back and forth along the second floor breezeway, whispering intently to herself. I eased myself into Malloy's car and locked the doors. The interior of his car still smelled like him and that hurt in a numb, abstract kind of way. I had to adjust the seat way forward to reach the pedals.

Pulling out of the parking lot, I had no idea where I was going. No solid plan, no clever scheme, nothing. I just drove.

I got on the 101 and drove west. Maybe Malloy had been right after all. Maybe the best thing to do really would be to get the hell out of Dodge. Keep on driving until I hit San Francisco and then get on a plane to anywhere. Leave all this madness behind.

But I couldn't have done it then any more than I could have done it the night before. I had to get Ridgeway or die trying. That's when I remembered Jesse's cell phone.

I pulled off the freeway and into the parking lot of an In-N-Out Burger. It only took a second of scrolling through the stored numbers to find one for Uncle Alan.

I spent the next hour opening and closing the little phone. I felt ashamed by how badly I wanted Malloy to be there, to light up a cigarette and squint and then let me know what we ought to do.

In the end, I went ahead speed-dialed the number.

"Christopher," Ridgeway said as soon as he picked up. "Where the hell are you? I've just about had it with this blasé incompetence of yours. I ask you to take care of a single 115-pound bimbo and you can't even do that right. I think we need to have a serious talk about your position in this organization."

My heart was beating wildly in my chest. I could barely catch my breath to speak.

"I'm sorry," I said. "Jesse can't come to the phone right now. Would you like to leave a message?"

There was a long pause on the other end of the line. I could hear him smoking.

"Angel?" Ridgeway asked.

"Yeah," I said.

"How nice to hear from you," he replied. "Where is that useless nephew of mine, anyway?"

"Never mind that," I told him. "What you want to ask is where's your money."

"All right," he said. "Where's my money."

"I have it right here," I said. "If I give it back, then this business with you and me is done, right?"

"Now you're finally being sensible," he said. "All I ever wanted was what was rightfully mine."

"Meet me in the lot behind 2372 Saco Street. You know the place, don't you? It's where your useless nephew didn't kill me."

"Right," he said. "I know it."

"Meet me there at midnight tonight," I said. "Come alone."

I ended the call and turned the phone off.

I sat there, gripping the wheel for what felt like forever. My whole body was shaking, my stomach roiling. Midnight? Why the fuck did I say midnight? That was sixteen hours away. I couldn't imagine what the hell I was going to do with myself for sixteen hours.

The hours passed. I drove around. Bought food and didn't eat it. Bought shoes and tossed the broken-heeled boots. Stared at the bland, familiar Valley mini-mall landscape.

It wasn't too late to blow town, but I didn't. I waited until midnight.

My plan, such as it was, was a simple one. I was going to plug Ridgeway as soon as I saw him. I didn't care if he had snipers secretly covering him. Let them shoot me after I shot him. At least the son of a bitch would beat me to hell.

Just before I got on the freeway to head downtown, I opened up the duffel bag on the seat beside me. My blue cup was broken into three pieces. The little robot was broken too, its smiling head and one arm detached from the dented body. My own little stack of cash was gone, probably still sitting on the nightstand at the Palmview where I'd left it. All I had left now was the Lakers t-shirt I didn't want to wear because it reminded me of Lia, the gun I used to kill Jesse, and Ridgeway's money. In a way that seemed weirdly fitting. I threw out the broken things in a 7-Eleven trashcan, traded my current garbage-stained t-shirt for the Lakers shirt and stuck the gun into the waistband of my jeans.

I got to the abandoned warehouse an hour and fifteen minutes early. There was no one there. I parked Malloy's car over near the *mercado* and then cautiously walked back to the meeting place. The money was way heavier than you'd think just money would be, but the walk was still much easier than the last time I'd traveled this route.

There was still nobody in sight. The run-down industrial neighborhood was just as deserted now as it had been on the day Jesse shot me, but I still felt like I had a neon sign over my head that read I HAVE A BAG FULL OF HUNDRED DOLLAR BILLS!!!

I made it to the lot without incident. No one else was there. So I waited. In a way, the waiting seemed almost worse than getting shot. All the second-guessing, the doubts, all the bullshit running through my head. But I wanted so badly to be that badass avenging angel, so there I was. Waiting.

In the end, it wasn't Ridgeway who showed up. It was the weasel. Lia's boyfriend. Vukasin.

"What the fuck?" I said to him as he rounded the corner into the lot. I pulled out the gun and drew a bead on the center of his chest. "I told your boss to come alone."

"Hello, Angel," he said, smiling. He was wearing an expensive, new leather trench coat over yet another awful shirt. "Nice haircut."

"Fuck you," I said. "You get your boss on the phone and you tell him the deal is off without him."

"I would," Vukasin said, talking a smiling step closer to me. "But you see, I forgot to charge my cell phone. How stupid of me."

"Stay the fuck away from me," I warned.

"You really will shoot me now, won't you?" he said, cocking his head and stepping back. "Our little girl is all grown up, eh?"

I caught a quick flicker in his gaze as it darted to my left and then back to my face. Alarms went off all through my body and I spun to the left just in time to meet something hard and heavy slamming into my temple. The smug and mocking thought that chased me down into blackness was...*some avenging angel*.

30.

I came to in another trunk. This one was much nicer than the Civic, better than the Sebring even, but it still sucked. I was bound and gagged, again. My head hurt worse than it had ever hurt before and I felt a drowsy kind of spinning sickness that made me wish I were already dead.

What the fuck was I thinking, trying to be some kind of badass tough guy? I was a porn star for Christ's sake, not a Green Beret. I could almost see Malloy shaking his head, smirking and making some deadpan comment about the shit I'd gotten myself into now. I hated him in that moment, for making me need him and then leaving me.

The car I was in eased into a slow stop. Footsteps came around to the rear and I cringed as the trunk lid sprang open. There would be no hesitation from Vukasin if he decided to pop a cap in my bitch ass.

But the person who opened the trunk wasn't Vukasin. Presumably it was the man who had cold-cocked me back in the lot behind that warehouse. I figured he must be the replacement for that blonde redneck thug Malloy had killed back in Vegas. This one was younger and better looking, his dark hair meticulously gelled into trendy dishevelment. The body under his basic black outfit was built more like a model than a power lifter but he lifted me out of the trunk and slung me over his broad shoulder easily and without comment.

Hanging upside down with my cheek pressed against the thug's back, I saw that the car whose trunk had been so nice was a slick black Chrysler 300. I was getting to be a regular trunk connoisseur. I made a mental note to request the Chrysler 300 for all future abductions.

I also saw that we were behind one of those awful, trashy post-war apartment complexes that fill the low-income neighborhoods of the northern Valley. Grimy stucco. Chipped paint. Indistinguishable from hundreds of others throughout Southern California.

Vukasin was there, holding my duffel bag and talking on a cell phone.

"Yes," he said into the phone. "I've got her and I've got the money." He looked over at me. "Yes, I understand."

He ended the call and gestured to the man holding me.

"Boss says we meet him at Sneaky Pete's on West 98th by LAX," Vukasin said, putting the duffel bag into the trunk in my place and slamming the lid. "He said it's right next door to the meet. You load up the outgoing girls, drive out to the meet, park the van behind the warehouse and then go over and meet the boss at Pete's. I'll deal with Angel myself."

"But I thought the boss said he wanted her included with the outgoing," the thug said, adjusting me on his shoulder.

"She will be," Vukasin said. "Only she and I have a few things we need to discuss together first."

He caught my eye and winked.

The thug carried me through a security gate and up some stairs and then stood in front of a unit on the second floor. The place was a standard low-rent garden apartment complex, all the units facing a central garden if by "garden" you meant a single rickety bench and some weedy dirt. The interior was not visible from the street. You could do pretty much anything you wanted here and no one would see it.

Vukasin unlocked the door. Inside wasn't a normal apartment. It was a crummy little dungeon. Bad fake stone pattern painted on the grubby walls. Rickety wooden equipment slopped thick with matte black paint. A large X bolted to one wall and studded with eyelets. A thinly padded bench with locking steel cuffs dangling from each of its four legs. Cheap, skinny floggers and flimsy paddles hanging from nails driven unevenly into the far wall. There were stains on the carpet that I didn't care to study. I thought of Ulka and her classy set-up and wondered what she would have thought about this place.

"Just put her down anywhere," Vukasin said.

The thug obliged by dumping me on the carpet at the foot of the X and quickly making himself scarce. One of the stains that I didn't want to think about was now an inch from my nose.

I wondered, were all the other units in this grim complex done up as cheesy fantasy sets like this one? Was this where they shot all the *Naughty Teens* videos? Did the girls turn tricks here too?

Alone with Vukasin now, I quickly assessed my situation. I was lying on my side. My hands were bound behind my back with a single short piece of nylon rope. Ditto my ankles. I was tightly gagged with a knotted handkerchief that dug deep into the corners of my mouth.

Vukasin hung his leather trench coat on a hook by the door and then squatted down beside me and pushed up my Lakers shirt, exposing my breasts. I had not had time to bind them down when I bolted from the Palmview and anyway at this late date it had seemed kind of beside the point to continue with the drag charade.

"You are really much too old for me, Angel," he said, gripping my breast and giving it a painful shake. "But you intrigue me. Your friend Zandora, she was intriguing too. For a time."

He reached behind my head and unknotted the gag, pulling the wet fabric from my mouth. He abruptly yanked me upright so that I was balanced on my knees, facing him. Pulling a straight razor from his pocket, he swiftly cut away my t-shirt, nicking the skin beneath more than once in the process. It was enough to pull me out of the stupor I'd been in. I had pretty much resigned myself to being shot; I'd even managed to convince myself that it would be a noble, tough guy kind of a death. But slow death by straight razor is a whole different ballgame.

Once my shirt was out of the way, Vukasin wrapped one skinny arm around me and kissed me, mashing my sore lips into my teeth like an eager teenager. I let him, focusing everything I had into working my wrists loose. They wouldn't give and wouldn't give and then suddenly the rope went miraculously slack, just enough to slip one hand free.

I had one shot. I remembered that tacky shirt he'd worn in Vegas, the one with the cards and dice on it, and I remembered the pistol I'd found under it, tucked down the back of his pants. He was wearing a different tacky polyester shirt today, but it was untucked the same way. I could only hope that he was a creature of habit.

When he reached down to unbutton my jeans, I made my move. The pistol was right where I'd hoped it would be. In less than a heartbeat, I had it out of his waistband and up under his chin.

"Get the fuck off me," I told him.

He dropped the razor and backed away slowly, eyes narrow and furious. I could see that he no longer harbored any doubt that I would shoot him.

"Back up," I told him, keeping the gun pointed at his face.

No snappy banter now. No back talk. He just stepped backwards toward the chintzy little bondage bench.

"Lie on your stomach and cuff your wrists to the bench," I said. He fastened one cuff around a wrist and then ineffectually fumbled, one handed, with the remaining cuff.

I freed my ankles and cuffed his remaining wrist and ankles to the bench myself. I put my spit-damp gag into his mouth, knotting it securely behind his head and then took his keys from his pocket. I took his trench coat too, since the sliced up Lakers t-shirt was a total loss. I put his gun in the deep pocket and grabbed an extra set of handcuffs and a roll of thick, heavy-duty electrical tape. Just in case.

I could have killed him without thinking twice. It wouldn't have troubled me at all. But it also wouldn't have satisfied me. No point wasting my time on wiping out all the rest of Ridgeway's little errand boys. Ridgeway was the one who planned this whole mess. Ridgeway was the one who needed to pay.

Outside in the thick unnatural stillness of the deserted complex, I stood with Vukasin's keys in my hand. I could get out of town in just the trench coat and my jeans, but if I was going to get Ridgeway, I needed clothes. If the girls were shooting videos and turning tricks here, they probably had a wardrobe room somewhere in this complex. In her scene for *Naughty Teens 17*, Lia had worn a sleazy hot pink hooker dress, but some of the other Naughty Teens had been in nondescript GND outfits so I was hoping I'd be able to find something besides stripper-wear and cheerleader costumes.

The first few doors I opened led to more sets. A schoolroom, an office, a prison with little wooden cells. By far the creepiest was a little girl's bedroom, complete with cute plush animals and a pink canopy bed. There were also a few minimally furnished studio apartments that looked like trick pads. All of them were empty.

I went downstairs to try some of the doors on the first floor. The locks on these doors were expensive and new, and there was more than one on each door. The first door I unlocked led to what I initially mistook for an empty apartment. There was no furniture in the room I could see from the front door, yet the lights were on. I was about to shut the door and try another when a blonde head peered around the doorless entry to a second room on the left.

"Hello?" I said.

A girl came out into the main room. She was naked. She had a pretty face but was clearly exhausted and her skinny, underdeveloped body was mottled with bruises and scratches. She made no attempt to cover herself. Her eyes were skittish, like Lia's had been. She didn't say anything.

"Do you speak English?" I asked.

Her lack of response answered for her, but at the sound of my voice, two other girls appeared behind her.

They were also naked, and also didn't seem to care. Any dignity or shyness had long since worn away. They were silent, resigned.

I quickly searched the tiny unit and found absolutely nothing inside. No clothes, no furniture, no toiletries, nothing at all. Just these three naked girls.

It was a pretty smart set-up Ridgeway had going here. This was the perfect place to keep illegal girls locked down tight, providing privacy for the johns and the shoots. In a neighborhood like this, nobody thought twice about heavy security bars and multiple locks. The neighbors would never imagine all that security wasn't to keep people out but to keep them in.

I went down the row of doors, opening them one after the other. The girls were housed three per unit, fifteen total. They were all pale and scared and painfully young. I would have been very surprised if even half of them were over eighteen. The girls were all naked and there were no clothes or shoes in any of their units. Not so much as a blanket or a towel. There was something hideously brilliant about keeping them demoralized that way, leaving them naked, making them sleep on the floor.

It took a lot of non-verbal coaxing to get them all out of their little carpeted prisons.

"Does anybody speak English?" I asked, once I had herded all the shivering girls into the central garden.

"Yes," a tall, awkward brunette replied.

"A little bit," said a bottom-heavy blonde, indicating a little bit between her thumb and forefinger.

"Okay," I said speaking slow and clear. "Where are clothes?"

The brunette pointed to a left corner unit on the

ground floor. When I unlocked the door, I found a dressing room filled with racks of slutty dresses and costumes. It was not unlike the Sissy Boudoir at Ulka's except the clothes were in smaller sizes.

"Everyone get dressed," I said.

The girls obediently did as I asked and the ones who didn't understand followed the examples of the ones who did. They were so used to doing what they were told that it made me angry.

I had hoped there would be some plain good-girl outfits but if there were any, they kept them somewhere else.

"Okay, I said. "Everyone dressed?"

I surveyed my little hooker army. Each girl was clad in a trashy spandex dress and plastic platform shoes or vinyl hot pants and a halter top. It was so preposterous that you had to laugh, but I suddenly thought of one particular motherfucker who would not be laughing when he saw them.

I led the girls up to the dungeon where Vukasin was manacled. In my absence, he had struggled so fiercely that he'd knocked the bench over on its side. His wrists were bleeding, but he had been unable to free himself.

I bent down to retrieve the open straight razor from the carpet and handed it to the blonde who understood English a little bit. She didn't need her English to understand what I had in mind. I was pleased to see, finally, flashes of defiance and life in fifteen pairs of eyes as understanding swept over the girls on a tide of foreign whispers.

As I turned away, I could hear Vukasin's muffled, impotent squeaks through the gag and frantic thumping as he struggled to get away from what he had coming. I left the girls to their revenge. I had my own to think about.

On my way out, I stopped off in the wardrobe room. The bare bones of a plan were starting to take shape in my mind. I ditched my dirty jeans and wiggled into a g-string bikini with easy-off plastic clasps. Over the bikini I pulled on a shiny black stretch vinyl minidress. There was a plastic toolbox filled with Wet N Wild 99-cent make-up. I quickly slapped on a thick layer of war paint and topped it off with a cherry red Bettie Page-style wig. I jammed my feet into sky-high stripper heels and then covered it all up with Vukasin's leather trench coat. The coat still smelled like him. It made me feel completely the opposite of the way wearing Malloy's coat had made me feel.

As I turned to go, I found myself facing a full-length mirror. Looking in that mirror, I suddenly knew my plan would work. I understood exactly what I had been doing wrong. All this time I'd been trying to be some kind of action movie tough guy. I'd tried to be Malloy with tits and look where it got me. There was only one way I was going to get Ridgeway. It was the only way I knew. A girl's gotta use her natural skills.

31.

Sneaky Pete's is to Eye Candy what your local taco truck is to Spago. Cheap, nasty and lowbrow. Full nude and no holds barred. I never danced there; frankly, you can hardly call what the girls do there "dancing."

As I pulled into the lot beside the sleazy little edifice, I checked my new face in the rearview mirror. I straightened the glossy red wig on my head, touched up my black cherry lips and pressed down my the corners of my false eyelashes. There was no time to spare. Only twenty minutes till closing.

I went inside and asked to see the manager. There was a familiar stink inside of sweat and baby oil and dead-end lives. The men clustered in the shadows, nursing overpriced soft drinks and pretending not to notice one another. A tiny, flat-chested girl worked the single stage. She was a brunette with big eyes, hardly more than a child. Her hipbones were so sharp they looked painful. She wore nothing but a silver g-string and moved her skinny limbs with a slow, spacey grace, like she was underwater. Van Halen's "Little Dreamer" crackled through the cheap speakers.

"Yeah?" the manager said, appearing suddenly at my elbow. "You looking for work?"

He was a burly biker right out of central casting. Beard. Ponytail. Beer gut. Tattoos. He looked like one of the first three guys the hero has to fight before he can get to the real bad guy.

"I know it's late," I said, making my voice and posture all submissive and needy. "But I was hoping you'd let me audition tonight and then if you like me…" I gave a shy little smile and fingered a strand of red synthetic hair. "Maybe you can give me some shifts this weekend."

"No problem, sugar," he said with a gap-toothed grin. "You're up next. It's g-strings on the stage but you go full nude in the champagne rooms. Extras are up to you." He winked and gestured toward the DJ booth. "Go tell Lenny your name and what song you want to dance to."

I headed over to the DJ booth and that's when I saw Ridgeway, sitting along the rail on the far right flanked by two men. One was the messy-haired thug who had carried me into the dungeon and the other a guy I'd never seen. Shaved head, goatee, bad tattoos. I didn't care. I only had eyes for Ridgeway.

I felt that cold rush, that jittery crush-like feeling in my belly, and part of me wanted to bolt. Maybe I was crazy to think I could do this. But I'd never be able to live with myself if I didn't try. I stared at the back of Ridgeway's head like hate alone was enough to kill him. He didn't notice me.

"Hey," a voice said. "How you doing, beautiful?"

I turned toward the voice. It was the DJ, who, by some bizarre coincidence turned out to be the lanky hotdog with the braids who had come to help Thick Vic get Roxette out of Taylor's bathroom. I wondered if the eviction had been successful, or if Roxette was still in there digging into her leg with the bloody toothbrush. He clearly did not recognize me.

"Um, hi," I said, fooling with the belt on the trench coat.

"What's your name, little sister?" he asked.

I looked over at the back of Ridgeway's head. He put a bill on the stage at the dancer's feet and his men quickly followed suit. She smiled in a vague sort of way, like a ticket taker in a movie theater.

"Vendetta," I said. "My name's Vendetta."

"Okay, Vendetta," the DJ said with a grin. "What's your favorite song? I got both kinds of music, rock *and* roll."

I flipped through the CD wallet he handed me until I spotted a disk of *Highway To Hell* by AC/DC. I pointed to the track I wanted to dance to and headed over to the edge of the stage.

The tiny girl finished up in an awkward split and then gathered up her sweaty, rumpled bills and discarded bits of spandex.

"Let's hear it for Missy!" the DJ said over the crackly PA system. "Show Missy some love, boys."

The modest crowd clapped listlessly and a few threw in a bill or two.

"And remember, if you'd like to get to know Missy a little better, you can take this beautiful lady into one of our private champagne rooms for an unforgettable couch dance. Remember, you gotta to show the greenery if you want to see the scenery."

An unkempt, dandruffy older man immediately nabbed Missy and dragged her off to one of the private rooms in the back. It looked like there were four rooms back there. Two were currently unoccupied, judging by the open curtains.

"Now boys," the DJ announced. "Before you call it an evening, I've got a very special treat that's gonna send you off with a bang. We've got a smokin hot new entertainer here at Sneaky Pete's tonight. Gentlemen, I give you the luscious, the vivacious, *VENDETTA!*"

My music started and I did what I could to calm my crazy speeding heart. Then I climbed up onto the stage.

Funny how old habits never really die. Just like riding a bicycle. I grabbed the roll of paper towels and antibacterial cleanser thoughtfully provided by the management and quickly wiped down the length of the brass pole. Then I went to work.

I slithered slowly out of Vukasin's leather trench coat to the familiar hoots and whistles of masculine approval. I made sure to set the coat down carefully and not let the pistol in the right pocket clunk loudly against the stage. As I shook my moneymaker, grinding against the pole as if I'd never quit, I realized that Angel Dare wasn't dead after all. She was alive and well, and she was pissed.

I peeled off the dress and thrust my gyrating ass into the eager faces around me, working my way toward Ridgeway. The marks ate it up with two forks.

"If you want blood," Bon Scott's distinctive rusty-hinge howl bellowed through the cheap speakers, "you got it!"

By the time I made my way over to the corner of the stage in front of Ridgeway and his cronies, I was down to my g-string. There was a green snowdrift of dollar bills and fives around my clunky plastic heels.

I got down on my hands and knees and rolled my spine, undulating my ass inches from the bastard's nose. I watched him in the mirror on the back wall. He was staring, mesmerized, right between my cheeks, almost like if he stared hard enough, he'd see through the leopard-print spandex barrier between him and the good stuff. After everything he'd put me through, and everything I'd gone through to get here, it was kind of shocking to discover that the big bad boss was just a man like any other. I had been worried that he would recognize me, but it was clear that he was paying no attention whatsoever to anything above my tits. The two goons were equally preoccupied, but they didn't matter. It was as if Ridgeway and I were alone. Like there was no one else on the planet. I've never felt so intense a hunger for someone. Not even Jesse.

I flipped on my back and bounced my legs into a deep splayed V, then arched back up to my feet as the song ended. If that motherfucker wanted blood, he was going to get it.

I gathered up the bills and clothing without turning away from Ridgeway. His eyes never left my crotch. His face had gone dumb with lust. I had him.

I slipped the trench coat over my g-string and deftly dodged several amorous suitors, heading directly to where Ridgeway sat.

"Would you like to get to know me a little better, honey?" I asked, pitching my voice low and whisper-sexy, sliding my body catlike against his.

The goons, seeing their boss was otherwise engaged, moved away to give him some privacy. The messy-haired guy started chatting up the tired-looking waitress while the bald one headed for the john. After all, what kind of danger could a 115-pound bimbo possibly pose?

"I'd love to," Ridgeway replied, running a sweaty

hand over my thigh. "But I'm afraid I've got a prior commitment."

"You can't spare even ten little minutes," I asked, brushing my bare breasts against his chest. "I swear I'll make it worth your while."

"I don't like pushy women," he said, mouth a tight line and suddenly chilly.

"You'll like me," I said, putting my arm around his waist and pressing the muzzle of the gun into his belly through the pocket of the trench coat. "What do you say?"

He said nothing but his body language told me he had finally recognized me. The messy-haired goon's back was turned. The bald goon was still in the bathroom. I could see Ridgeway's pulse ticking in the soft spot beneath his ear. This was where it could all go to hell in a heartbeat.

"All right," he finally said, getting slowly to his feet.

He let me lead him back to one of the two available champagne rooms.

Despite its classy name, the champagne room was actually a dingy cubicle with a cheap futon on a folding metal frame that looked like it had been scavenged from the trash outside a college dorm. I didn't even want to think about all the bodily fluids that soaked into that futon over the course of any given shift. Luckily, there would be no couch dances tonight.

"Pull the curtain," I told Ridgeway.

He did what I asked in hostile silence. There was a dull, monotonous rhythm of thumps and groans filtering through from the next cubicle.

"You're not going to get away with this," he said.

"That's funny," I replied. "That's what your nephew said right before I killed him." I tossed him the cuffs. "Sit down and cuff your hands around that." I gestured at one of the futon's tubular metal legs.

He caught the cuffs against his chest and fastened them around one wrist, eyes never leaving mine.

"You can't get out of here alive," he told me as he slowly lowered himself onto the futon. "You shoot me, everyone in the place will hear it."

"Other wrist," I told him. "Put the cuff through the edge of the frame—no, behind that piece. That's right. Now cuff your other wrist."

He did what I said, eyes narrow. This left him slouched down with his cuffed wrists locked between his knees, trapped in place by the frame of the futon. He wasn't going anywhere.

"Why are you doing this, Angel?" he asked. "Why didn't you just run with the money?"

"You don't get it, do you?" I asked. "This is not just about me. It's about Didi. About Malloy. About Sam."

"Sam?" He shook his head. "Please. Sam sold you out, Angel. He set you up to save his own ass. You ought to be glad he's dead."

Ridgeway was just fucking with me, trying to get me to make a mistake.

"Bullshit," I said. "He told me you had Georgie."

But then I thought of seeing Georgie on the news, flanked by cops. I'd wondered then what had really happened and I was wondering now. Was it true? Had Sam set me up?

"People say all kinds of things," Ridgeway said. "I bet Malloy said he would love you forever, right? Until he took off with the money. Or tried to, anyway."

Malloy had never promised me anything like that.

Ridgeway was grasping at straws, blindly groping for buttons to push and missing.

"You don't know shit about Malloy," I told him. "Or me."

"Maybe not," Ridgeway said, speaking casually like he didn't have a gun pointed at his face. "But I know plenty about Sam. I know he loved girls with big tits. I also know he threw money at girls with big tits. A lot of money. Bought them pretty things, paid all their bills. Sam was in over his head when I offered to help him out. He just helped me out in return. Nothing personal, Angel."

Of course I didn't like hearing it all spelled out like that. It hurt to know that someone I'd thought of as a friend had sold me out. That I had been betrayed yet again. For money. Always for money.

But Ridgeway failed to realize that I had been hurt so much, so often, in so short a span of time, that in that particular moment, I couldn't feel a thing. Later, when this was done and I had time to go over and over it in my head, I knew it would hurt plenty. Sam, Malloy, everything. But right now I felt weightless and ice cold. I had nothing left. I was finally the avenging angel I'd wanted to become all along.

"Alan," I said. "No more talk."

I traded the gun for the roll of electrical tape.

When I had a few layers of shiny black tape wrapped around his head from chin to upper lip, I paused. For some reason, I had never noticed the color of his eyes before. They were blue, like Jesse's. Scared like Jesse's. I looked into his eyes, smoothed the tape over his mouth with my thumb and then continued wrapping the tape around his head.

When I covered his nostrils, he went wild on the futon, bucking and twisting as he tried to wrench his hands free of the cuffs or the cuffs free of the metal frame. Next door the thumping sped up, moans louder now and heading into the home stretch. Ridgeway's desperate struggles didn't sound all that different.

I stepped back and watched the kaleidoscope of emotion in his wide eyes until the show was over.

32.

Ridgeway was dead for nearly a full minute before the action next door reached a noisy crescendo. I pulled my gaze away from where he lay, cuffed and slumped over, his face purple above the electrical tape. I squeezed back into the vinyl dress and got the hell out of there.

When I left the champagne room, Ridgeway's two thugs were back on the rail. They didn't look away from the stripper they were watching. Nobody noticed me as I slipped out through a side door.

I dumped the red wig in a bucket that had been designated for cigarettes but was rarely used, judging from the number of butts on the surrounding ground. The cool night air felt good on my sweaty scalp.

From where I stood, I could see through the chain link fence to the warehouse next door. There was a van parked in the warehouse lot. The windows were tinted but it didn't take much to picture the girls inside. The outgoing girls. The ones Ridgeway had used up and planned to dump like unwanted puppies that had outgrown their cuteness.

I thought again of Lia. Of everything she had gone through to stop what happened to her from happening to her little sister. That little sister, Ana, was probably in that building next door right now, waiting to be purchased like livestock. If Ridgeway no-showed, the men who'd smuggled Ana and the five other girls into the country would have no trouble finding another buyer.

This was not my problem. I was done. I'd had my revenge and Malloy was wrong. It wasn't empty. It was strange and scary but still sweet, just like I'd wanted it to be. I didn't know what I was going to do with my life now and frankly, I didn't care. It didn't matter. I'd won. No one had believed I could do it, not even me, but I had. I'd beat that bastard and made him pay for what he did to me. I was free. I had one hundred eighty thousand dollars in the trunk of Vukasin's car. So why couldn't I stop thinking about Lia?

Am I sorry about the choice I made? Do I ever wonder what my life would have been like if I had taken the money and fucked off to wherever? Sometimes, sure. I mean, I think about it. I've got to do something to pass the time.

But I couldn't just fuck off and leave them. I guess that makes me a softie or a sucker but I just couldn't let it go, any more than I could have let Ridgeway live. I walked over to Vukasin's car and got the duffel bag out of the trunk.

The warehouse next door apparently housed an operation that imported tropical fish from all over the world. Walking in through the open door, I was hit with this strange and powerful smell. Brine and fish and bleach. There was a guy with a machine gun waiting to greet me inside. A dour, bloodless shark in a good suit.

"Mr. Ridgeway sent me," I said, offering up the duffel bag like a sacrifice.

The door guard unzipped the bag for a quick look at

the contents. Then he nodded and reached out to undo the trench coat, rough hands sliding over the sides of my body. It took a minute to register the fact that he didn't want a date, he was just frisking me. He quickly found and pocketed Vukasin's gun.

"Go ahead," he said with a heavy accent. It sounded like Lia's.

I had no idea where I was supposed to go, but didn't want to ask for directions. Strolling along the shadowed rows of small water-filled Plexiglas cubes, I noticed that each cube held a single sad and gorgeous aquatic prisoner. They watched me, silent and goggle-eyed as I passed. I think even they knew I had no idea what I was doing. I made my way toward the only furnished area in the enormous warehouse space, a cluster of cheap folding chairs and a card table that held a coffee carafe and some plastic spoons.

Past the table was a doorway leading into some kind of carpeted office. There was a light inside. I couldn't think of what else to do, so I went in.

Inside the office were six girls and a man. The girls sat on a long couch, huddled together like nervous rabbits. They wore cheap dresses and looked dirty, with unwashed hair and sticky, sleepless eyes. The man was standing. He was older, tall, bald and stone cold. I could see war atrocities in his flat gray eyes. He seemed to be human shaped, with two arms and two legs and all the standard equipment, but there was nothing human about him at all. I got the feeling that this guy would watch a girl strip or watch her die with the same expression. There would be no manipulating this man with feminine wiles. My only chance here was to give him the money and hope for a fair deal.

I handed over the duffel. The man counted the money faster than a casino machine and gave a curt nod.

"Keys," he said, putting out his hand.

I froze. What keys? Was I supposed to have keys? I groped desperately through my brain for the answer that would keep me alive. Then I thought of the van. The van full of outgoing girls. That was the trade, right? One hundred and eighty thousand dollars plus six used girls for the six fresh ones. He clearly wanted the keys to that van. I didn't have them.

The gig was up. There was nothing I could do to trick this guy. No lie I could cobble together that would explain why I didn't have the keys to the van. I just shook my head, looked at the floor and waited to die.

Amazingly, I didn't. Instead of shooting me in the face, the man simply nodded, grabbed one of the girls off the sofa by the arm and left.

For a long time, I just stood there, staring at the five remaining girls. I was baffled by this turn of events until I realized it was just a cold-blooded display of sexual economics. When the six used girls were removed from the equation, the man had simply subtracted a single new girl from the deal. One fresh girl was worth six used ones. Unbelievable. I really hoped the girl he took back hadn't been Lia's sister.

"Ana?" I said, scanning the girls' thin and haggard faces for a family resemblance. "Ana Albu?"

A brunette in the middle said something I didn't understand. She couldn't have been older than fifteen and didn't look anything like Lia.

"Ana?" I asked again, pointing to her barely developed chest.

She nodded. "Ana," she said, pointing to herself.

I heard sirens. I still had no idea what the hell I was going to do.

33.

I suppose I could have made a run for it, but where could I go? What was I going to do once I got away? I had no money anymore. No clever plan. Everyone I cared about was dead. I was tired. Bone weary and close to total physical collapse. I had done what needed to be done and now I had absolutely nothing left.

I motioned for the girls to follow me. The door guard was gone. We were alone in the big echoing warehouse except for the rows and rows of beautiful sea creatures waiting to be sold like the girls had been.

Out back, the van full of used girls was still there. I could see red and blue lights from police prowlers swarming all around Sneaky Pete's. I guess I was getting better at breaking glass, because it only took one try to smash the passenger side window with my leather-wrapped fist.

I brushed fragments of safety glass from the front of the trench coat, popped the locks and opened the sliding back door. The girls inside didn't move or react at all.

They looked awful. Pale and scrawny, riddled with track marks and sores. Their lifeless eyes barely seemed to register my presence. They wore identical sweatpants, t-shirts from the 99-cent store and plastic flip flop sandals.

"Come on," I said. "Let's go."

Some of their heads turned toward my voice. Most

didn't. None of them got up or made any move toward the door.

"Come on, hurry," I said. I made to grab a scabby arm on the girl closest to the door and then lost my nerve.

I backed away from the van. The new girls behind me all looked at me, bewildered and unsure.

"All right then," I said. "Anyone who's coming…"

I left the van door open and headed back over to Sneaky Pete's. The new girls followed me but none of the ones from the van did.

There was a group of cops standing outside Sneaky Pete's talking to the manager.

"That's her!" the manager said, pointing a finger at me.

"Ma'am," a young black cop said, stepping cautiously forward while several of his pals drew down on me with guns and steely stares. "I'll need you to come with me."

"Sure," I said. "Have you got room in your squad car for all my friends?"

He eyed the nervous girls as he pulled a pair of handcuffs from his belt.

"And while you're at it," I told him as I let him cuff my hands behind my back. "A Romanian translator would probably be a big help. A doctor, too. There's six more in the van next door and fifteen out in the Valley."

Now that it was finally over, I felt nothing but a numb sort of relief. I couldn't find the energy to wonder about the future. About a trial and jail and the media circus and all the madness that I knew was waiting for me. All I knew was that in some weird way, I was glad I hadn't run. I was glad that, after all the different people I had been forced to be, I could be myself again. I could be Angel Dare again.

I'd take the rap for Jesse and Ridgeway fair and square, but I'd fight tooth and nail against Ridgeway's kiddie porn frame-up and I'd beat it if it killed me. I'd never be able to go back to the business, but hell, maybe I'd end up even more famous by the time this was done. I'd go from "Didn't she used to be…?" to "That's her, that's Angel Dare." Maybe it wasn't exactly the type of fame I'd always wanted, but hey, no publicity is bad publicity, right? Isn't that what they say?

The cop who cuffed me read me my rights and asked if I understood. I told him that I did and that I wanted to talk to Detective Erlichman.

"What do you want to talk to Erlichman for?" he asked, maneuvering me none too gently toward a waiting squad car.

"He'll want to talk to me," I told the cop.

"Why is that?" he asked, grasping the curve of my shorn head and pushing me down into the back seat of the cruiser.

I looked up at him, at all the cops and reporters, the bikers and gawkers gathered around to see what all the excitement was about.

"I'm Angel Dare," I said.

I can't say the look on the cop's face made it all worth it, but it sure made me smile.

THE
END